ALL GOOD
Gifts

ALL GOOD Gifts

KATHLEEN MORGAN

Fleming H. Revell

A Division of Baker Book House Co
Grand Rapids, Michigan 49516

Published by Fleming H. Revell
a division of Baker Book House Company
P.O. Box 6287, Grand Rapids, MI 49516-6287
www.bakerbooks.com

Printed in the United States of America

Library of Congress Cataloging-in-Publication Data is on file at the Library of Congress, Washington, D.C.

ISBN 0-8007-1852-6

Scripture is taken from the King James Version of the Bible.

Scripture marked NLT is taken from the *Holy Bible*, New Living Translation, copyright © 1996. Used by permission of Tyndale House Publishers, Inc., Wheaton, IL 60189. All rights reserved.

To my sister Diane

To those who use well what they are given, even more will be given, and they will have an abundance. But from those who are unfaithful, even what little they have will be taken away.

Matthew 25:29 NLT

Prologue

It was another typical day in the life of a New York City plastic surgeon. Three patients had cancelled. Two more had called as soon as the office opened, demanding same-day appointments, and so far half who *had* made their appointments had been fifteen to twenty minutes late.

Dr. Devra MacKay finished skimming her new patient's chart with a small, inward sigh, closed it, and looked up to meet the woman's gaze from across her desk. "Your lab, chest-ray, and EKG results are all normal, Mrs. Mathison. I think it's time to get you on the schedule for your blepharoplasty. Will some time after the first of the year work for you?"

Dottie Mathison pursed her thin lips, setting off a cascade of tiny wrinkles around her mouth. Some dermabrasion or a skin peel was in order, Devra thought. Should she suggest it be added to the eyelid surgery, or save that discussion for the post-op visit?

One glance at her desk clock sealed Devra's decision. She was behind enough as it was. Best wait until post-op.

"Definitely after the first of the year," Dottie replied at last. "Too much is going on this month with Christmas and all the parties." She arched a perfectly penciled brow. "How do you find the time even to see patients yourself in December, Dr. MacKay? Aren't you on the Breast Cancer Foundation board *and* a member of Lincoln Center's Junior Committee? I know both of them always throw big holiday bashes."

Devra smiled. "Yes, I am. But my patients always come—"

The light on her desk phone began a frenetic flashing. It was Susan Webster, the office receptionist. Devra met Mrs. Mathison's gaze. "Would you excuse me for a moment? Seems my receptionist needs something."

Dottie nodded. "Of course, Doctor."

Devra punched the button below the flashing light and picked up the phone. "Yes, Susan?"

"I've got good news and bad news. Your 2:30 appointment this afternoon just cancelled, so after Mathison you're back on schedule and even have time for lunch."

With only the greatest of efforts, Devra squelched the impulse to roll her eyes. "And is that the good or the bad news?"

Susan gave a sharp, staccato laugh. "The good news, of course. The bad news is Eleanor Davis has called an emergency meeting of the Junior Committee for tomorrow night. Something about the caterer cancelling out at the last minute, and since you're part of the social committee . . ."

Tomorrow night was the Bradfords' Christmas dinner too. Though held later than usual this year, since it was already the eighteenth of December, the dinner was as much a charitable event as a social one. Each seat at the always elegant, twenty-foot table went for the princely sum of five hundred dollars, money that was promptly donated to a halfway house for abused women. On many levels, it was money well spent. Devra usually picked up several new patients every year at the Bradfords' dinner.

"See what time Eleanor wants me at the meeting," she said. "I want to be at the Bradfords' no later than 8:00 P.M. sharp. And I need to allow a half hour to get there, considering the distance between the two places."

"Okay, I'll ask her." Once more, Susan's startling laugh echoed through the phone. "But since Mrs. Davis isn't on the Bradfords' guest list anymore, I'm not sure she's going to take much pity on you."

Devra sighed. Sometimes all the high-society infighting got to be a bit much. There wasn't anything she could do about it, though, so she tried to stay out of it. No sense antagonizing potential patients by taking sides on what was, for the most part, rather silly, self-serving power struggles among some of the city's richest matrons. Matrons who were not only her bread and butter but also potential patrons with the clout to open up coveted positions of power in New York City's medical community.

"Just do the best you can, Susan." Once again, Devra's gaze strayed to the clock. "And be as circumspect as possible as to my reasons for having to be somewhere else tomorrow evening, will you?"

Susan chuckled. "You can count on it, boss." With that, her high-energy receptionist hung up.

"So, Mrs. Mathison"—Devra set her receiver back in its cradle—"I think everything's in order for the next step. Susan will make you two appointments—one for the actual procedure and one for a visit with our nurse, who'll finish up prepping you for the surgery. And if you ever feel, at any time, that you've a question Susan or my nurse can't answer to your satisfaction, you know you can always contact me."

Dottie clutched her expensive purse to her equally expensive tailored silk suit and stood. "I appreciate that, Dr. MacKay. You've an undeniable gift for this kind of work—everyone I know speaks of you in such glowing terms—and I'm so pleased you were finally able to fit me into your busy schedule. I've heard so much about the personal touch you offer your patients. Believe me, it's so refreshing after all those years of being treated like some piece of meat on an assembly line."

Devra pushed back her chair and stood. "Well, we work hard here to prevent that. And we're always open to patient feedback at any time."

Dottie smiled and nodded. "Most certainly, Dr. MacKay."

After seeing her patient to the door, Devra headed back to her desk. She sat and absentmindedly ran her fingers through her short blond curls. Time for a trim, before the whirlwind round of Christmas festivities began, she thought. Now, what was the name of that exclusive salon Eleanor Davis had raved about?

Devra's thoughts turned to tomorrow's social committee meeting. Knowing Susan's propensity for hoof-in-mouth disease at times, Devra decided to forestall any problems by making the call herself. Susan was an excellent receptionist, but Ellie Davis could be quite inquisitive if she scented any possibility for gossip.

The phone light flashed brightly. Devra's hand stilled in midair. *Not another good news/bad news scenario,* she prayed. She punched down on the button.

"What's it now, Susan? It'd better be that my next patient is ready and waiting out there."

"Call from Culdee Creek Ranch on line one." The receptionist's voice was clipped and all business now. "Some man named Ross Blackstone, and he says it's an emergency. I thought you'd better take it."

A premonition rippled through Devra. *Daddy. Something's happened to Daddy.*

She pushed the button for line one and lifted the receiver to her ear. "Hello? Ross? What's the matter?"

"It's your father, Devra. Logan's had a massive heart attack. . . . He's gone, Devra."

one

As United Airlines flight 7689 dropped its flaps and landing gear, the jet gave a soft, subtle jerk backward. Devra closed the novel she'd been trying to lose herself in for nearly the entire flight and shoved it into the side pocket of her leather purse. With eyes bleary and burning from a sleepless night and bouts of weeping, she gazed down on the winter-browned, rolling landscape east of Colorado Springs.

In past flights home for her annual Christmas visit, this particular moment had always filled her with a heady anticipation. Soon the plane would land and she'd disembark to find her father, Logan MacKay, and sometimes even their housekeeper, Thelma McCune, waiting for her outside the security checkpoint. The broad smiles that would brighten their expressions when they first caught sight of her never failed to warm Devra's heart. It made the trip worth every penny of the first-class seating and the two weeks of lost income when putting her lucrative plastic surgery practice on hold.

This year, however, there'd be no beloved father awaiting her. Though Colorado Springs boasted some fine cardiologists and cardiac surgeons, nothing could be done for her father. He had died before the EMS ambulance could even reach him.

"At least your dad died on the ranch he loved," Ross had offered yesterday on the telephone in an attempt to console her. Devra's mouth twisted sourly. Only men obsessed with ranching, as both Ross Blackstone and her father had always been, would find comfort in that. All she could think of was that maybe if her father had lived closer to the city hospital, he would've had a chance.

Still, considering there was little love lost between her and Culdee Creek's foreman, Devra supposed she would have received anything Ross said poorly. She didn't like the man. He was just too arrogant and self-centered. And he treated her—even now, seventeen years after he had first

16

sauntered onto Culdee Creek looking for a job—like some kid wet behind the ears.

He'd soon get what was coming to him, Devra vowed. The tables had turned. Though she would've wished it otherwise, she was now owner of Culdee Creek and he was just another hired man.

The plane's wings tipped, angling the huge aircraft into its final approach. From her window, she caught a brief glimpse north to the dark swatch of forest stretching from the Front Range for miles east until it dwindled into the rolling hills of the high plains. Culdee Creek was up there, nestled at the edge of the Black Forest. Her heart twisted.

Culdee Creek . . . home. But now a home without a mother *or* father.

Tears burned her eyes, and with a fierce, almost angry effort, Devra blinked them back. Tears were a sign of weakness. She had learned that all too well in the days of her medical training. And when it came to her pending encounter with Ross Blackstone, she didn't want to show any signs of weakness.

For one final instant, Devra allowed her anger at him to flame hot and bright, then squelched that too. She'd deal with him later. What mattered now was her father, getting through his funeral, dealing with the cards and condolences, sorting through his possessions, and putting everything to right. One day at a time was all she could manage, and Ross Blackstone was hardly high up there on her list of priorities.

The plane was rapidly losing altitude now. Devra focused on the ground rising up to meet them. She leaned back in her seat, tightened her safety belt an extra notch, and closed her eyes. It was time to turn off the emotions and just do what needed to be done.

two

*H*olding his black Stetson, he stood on the far side of the airport security checkpoint, dressed in a green-and-blue plaid flannel shirt, navy blue down vest, jeans, and his usual scuffed boots. In spite of her best efforts, Devra's heart lurched when she saw Ross Blackstone. Try as she might, she had never gotten over her childhood attraction to Culdee Creek's darkly handsome foreman.

When he had first come to Culdee Creek, Ross had been a twenty-one-year-old man down on his luck and looking for anything that might pay him a wage. He had assured

Logan MacKay that he knew his way around horses and could break anything remotely related to an equine. Logan soon put the ebony-haired, brown-eyed young man to the test. A test Ross had passed with flying colors when he managed to stay on Mad Mo, Culdee Creek's "I'd sooner buck than do most anything except eat" piebald gelding, until the wily animal had finally tired of his game and trotted off with his rider still astride.

That feat was enough to win fifteen-year-old Devra's heart. In the ensuing weeks of almost daily contact with Ross, who mysteriously refused to share much of his past with anyone, she found herself tongue-tied when she was near him and daydreaming about him when she wasn't. Of course, in those days all her emotions resided in that crazy vortex of incredible highs and lows, mostly because of the loss of her mother only six months earlier in a car crash and the belated but intense surge of feminine hormones that unfortunately coincided with Ross's arrival.

She would've given her heart—and love—to him, if only he had let her. Instead, when Devra had finally summoned the courage to write Ross her first love letter, his response had been unexpectedly cruel. He had no time for little girls, he had coldly informed her, then dropped the letter at her feet and walked away.

Not one word about that painful incident had ever been broached by either of them again. Most likely her heart-wrenching admission had meant nothing to him. It had, however, been devastating to her. To this day, she hadn't completely recovered from the rejection, or forgiven him.

So why, she wondered as she plastered on a social smile and strode resolutely toward him, after all this time and the undeniable success she had made of her life, did the memory of that teenage heartbreak still bother her? And why did she still manage to find such an arrogant, tactless, mean-spirited man attractive? There was only one explanation. She definitely had a screw loose somewhere.

"Hey, blue eyes. It's good to see you again," Ross said in his usual patronizing greeting when she finally joined him. "I just wish you were visiting for a different reason."

"How're things at Culdee Creek?" she replied through gritted teeth as they turned and resumed the trek to the baggage-claim area. Why did he insist on calling her "blue eyes"? How childish!

He sighed. "Not so good, I'm afraid. Everyone's still in shock. But who wouldn't be? This time two days ago, Logan was tossing bales of hay from a flatbed truck up into the barn's storage loft, and tossing them as fast and furiously as the rest of us."

She bit back a bitter reply. Maybe her father's heart would have held out a while longer if he hadn't been doing such strenuous work. Maybe if Ross had been doing his job as foreman, Culdee Creek's owner wouldn't have always felt compelled to help him out.

Devra knew, though, that no one could stop her father

from doing what he wanted to do. Not her, not Ross Black-stone, and not even precarious health—if her father had even realized how precarious his health really was.

"Dad never said anything to me about his heart." She shot Ross a slanting look. "Did you know something was wrong?"

The big foreman shrugged. "I knew he took a few pills, and had a doctor's appointment in town every few months or so. Logan kept the rest to himself, and I didn't pry."

"I wish you had."

Ross gave an emphatic nod. "So do I."

The flow of traffic ahead slowed as everyone either filed onto the escalator or headed down the stairs. When Devra and Ross's turn came, they took the stairs. Two minutes later, they stood by the luggage carousel and waited for her bags. It provided the perfect excuse not to talk, what with all the people crowding around and the need to watch for her luggage.

Devra was glad of it. She was too upset. Her feelings were in such a chaotic jumble, and she knew she was in danger of turning the brunt of it all on Ross. Not that he didn't deserve a lot of what she ached to unleash, but this wasn't the time or place.

Besides, tears were just as perilously close to the surface. She *would* stay in control. She just would.

It took a superhuman effort on Devra's part to contain herself, but Ross seemed oblivious to her torment. As she pointed out the various pieces of her designer luggage, he sprang, like some sporting dog retrieving a downed duck, toward one suitcase, then another, and finally to her much smaller overnight case.

"Should I get a cart, or do you think we can handle all my stuff together?" Devra asked when he triumphantly rejoined her with the last piece of luggage.

"Depends." The foreman's lips twitched minutely at each corner. "Can you carry your overnight case?"

She arched a thin, dark blond brow. "Funny thing. I was wondering the same about you."

Ross chuckled. "Never have gotten over that mile-wide competitive streak, have you?"

Devra stooped and picked up her overnight case. "In case you didn't know, wimps don't make it far in medical school."

His smile faded. "No, I don't suppose they do. But then, I never took you for a wimp, Devra. You've got too much of your father in you for that."

Devra fought the tears that threatened to fill her eyes. Strange how the mind could so easily forget, if only for a short while, such painful realities. Realities like a parent had just died, and you were now an orphan. Realities like you were home once more, and that home would never be the same again.

But then, she thought, the mind was a master at protecting itself. It was almost as if, in some instinctive way, it knew it could only bear a certain amount of intense grief before it sought relief, even if only temporarily.

There was no harm in it, she supposed. And it wasn't as if the price of such a loss wasn't still to be paid in weeks, months, and even years of suffering. It just wasn't paid all at once.

They hadn't far to walk, since Ross had parked the ranch pickup in the short-term parking lot. Which was probably for the best, Devra thought as a frigid wind whipped up almost as soon as they left the airport terminal's protective shelter. In spite of her thick, full-length black wool coat, she shivered.

"Welcome to Colorado," she groused, slinging her purse onto her shoulder and pulling up her coat collar. "Do you think you could've made it any colder?"

"It is a bit nippy, isn't it?" Ross paused, set down the suitcases, and quickly zipped his vest and flipped up its collar. "The weatherman said today's high would be about zero, with a wind chill that'd make it closer to ten below."

"Ten below!" Devra snuggled down even deeper into the relative warmth of her coat. "Whoever heard of it getting that cold this time of year?"

Ross shrugged. "Just one of those unseasonably chilly Decembers. We get them every once in a while. If we're lucky, maybe we'll even have a white—"

He stopped short. His lips went taut, and he stared straight ahead.

Devra knew what Ross was going to say. White Christmases weren't the norm here on the Front Range, even if it was Colorado. Not that either of them would've cared one way or another. This year, white or not, Christmas wasn't going to be merry or bright. As far as she was concerned, there wasn't any reason to celebrate Christmas at all.

They didn't say another word until they reached the pickup, loaded the luggage in the back, climbed in, and headed out of the airport parking lot. In fact, neither of them spoke until they had finally merged onto the fast-moving Powers Boulevard heading north.

Ross finally broke the heavy silence. "The funeral's planned for the day after tomorrow. Your father already had a mortuary picked out, as well as a casket, and, of course, he intended to be buried next to your mother in Grand View's cemetery."

Three generations of MacKays had been buried in the cemetery of the now nonexistent town of Grand View. It was a quaint old burial ground, nestled in the ponderosa pines five miles south and west of the former town. Until the late 1930s, Grand View had been a thriving town, boasting two churches, a school, a country store, a granary, a train depot, and quite a few other businesses and homes. Then in the flood of 1935 the railroad bed had been washed out and so badly destroyed that the railroad found it easier to divert the tracks toward Colorado Springs. That decision had sounded the town's death knell.

It was a miracle of sorts Culdee Creek had managed to

survive the loss of the railroad and the town's demise. But survive and even flourish it did, thanks to her family's hard work and countless innovations. Not that she particularly cared just now. For all practical purposes, Culdee Creek had killed her father. And it was hard to summon up much affection for a ranch she had chosen to leave in the pursuit of her dreams—and what was ultimately a far better life.

Devra finally forced herself to reply. "Yes, I figured he would've had everything worked out in advance. Daddy always was a very organized man. Is there anything left you'd like for me to do?"

"No. It's all been taken care of. All you need to do is attend the funeral and keep a stiff upper lip at the reception."

Somehow, that news didn't surprise her either. Ross was an equally disciplined and organized man. A control freak, if the truth be told, and yet another thing she disliked about him. He seemed to think he was still in charge—a fantasy she soon intended to demolish.

"There is one other thing, though, that I think you should know," Ross said, cutting into her less-than-charitable thoughts.

Devra turned in her seat toward him. "What's that? I thought you had everything taken care of."

"This has nothing to do with me. I didn't even know about it until this morning." He kept his gaze fixed on the road ahead, but she noted a subtle tightening of his grip on the steering wheel. "Do you remember Sam Dillon?"

Her thoughts raced. "Yes, I do. He was Dad's lawyer friend, wasn't he? Didn't he finally move to Denver?"

"He did. And he was more than Logan's friend. He was his attorney."

She was beginning to get the feeling she was being strung along. "Yes? And?"

"As you might expect, your father left a will. Sam wants us to meet with him the day after the funeral for the reading of it."

So what was the big deal? With or without a will, she was her father's only child. Everything would go to her.

"The day after the funeral's fine." Devra frowned. "Why does Sam want the both of us to meet with him, though? It's not like I need a baby-sitter."

"I haven't a clue." Ross signaled for a right turn as Powers neared Highway 24. "There was one thing Sam said that didn't make a whole lot of sense, though."

Here we go again, stringing me along, she thought in rising irritation. "Yes, and what was that?"

"Sam said the reason he needed us to meet with him was because the will wasn't as clear-cut as we might imagine. And that it concerned the both of us."

three

It never failed to amaze Devra, even with the psychological buffer of a once-yearly visit home, how quickly the countryside east of the Springs was being swallowed up—almost daily now, it seemed—by subdivisions and commercial businesses. Soon it would be nonstop houses from Colorado Springs east to as far as the small and still very rural town of Calhan. But then, it had been a running joke that the houses on the north/south corridor of Interstate 25 would soon stretch nonstop from the city of Pueblo to Colorado Springs and all the way to Denver.

She supposed she had no right to complain. After all, she lived in one of the world's biggest concrete jungles. But New York had been that way for probably a hundred years or more, while Colorado Springs had only begun suffering the effects of overdevelopment in the past fifteen years. The problem was that the sprawling growth had begun to impact even a ranch the size of Culdee Creek.

Traffic had increased until it took nearly double the time to get anywhere, thanks to a road system that had failed to keep up with the growing influx of cars and new inhabitants. And there was now fear among country folk that some of the aquifers flowing beneath the land might run dry, necessitating either a costly drilling into an even deeper aquifer or an imposed limit to the amount of water used for outdoor purposes, like watering gardens and livestock. People—especially city dwellers—couldn't seem to get it into their heads that this was arid land, high desert almost. Water wasn't inexhaustible like it was in some other parts of the country.

Devra looked at Ross as he drove along, effortlessly herding the big Ford pickup up Meridian Road toward the dark line of ponderosa pines marking the southernmost edge of the Black Forest. From the serene expression on his face, it appeared he was all but oblivious to the housing boom going on around him. In fact, she realized as she studied him, he looked as if he were praying, so calm was his expression.

She shouldn't be surprised. Ross had claimed a personal relationship with God for five or six years now, since that

Christmas Eve he had suddenly proclaimed he'd accompany Devra and her father to services at the Episcopal church in Colorado Springs.

Devra's mouth tightened in disdain. Well, no matter. She didn't believe that Ross Blackstone would ever change a single aspect of his supremely self-centered life—or himself—for the sake of anyone, especially God.

The realization that she was thinking about him again filled her with a renewed swell of irritation. She jerked her gaze to the passenger window, staring hard at the pine forest whizzing by. In the early years when her ancestors had first made Culdee Creek their home, the Black Forest had been called the Pinery and was the site of several logging companies. Indeed, the huge forest had been all but stripped clean over the course of years because of the demand for lumber in the Springs and Denver.

These days, just like her, the existing trees were second and third growth. Not the original stock, but an integral part of the land and continuing history nonetheless. A part that needed to survive, grow, and produce in its own time and way.

That concept was one her father hadn't understood. But how could he? For all his education and ability to accept and even use the things of today, Logan MacKay was a man who, at heart, had been born too late. His values were those of a courtly gentleman dedicated to preserving tradition. A man married to the land and fiercely loyal to God, home, and family. And because he loved Culdee Creek with all that was in him, her father could never seem to understand, much less accept, that Devra hadn't wanted to settle down, marry—at least any time soon—and give up her medical practice to eventually take over Culdee Creek.

That difference of opinion was the one source of dissension between them—excluding their ongoing difference of opinion over Ross—and it grated on Devra's nerves whenever she came home. To her father's credit, he never harped on the subject. The same, however, couldn't be said of Ross Blackstone.

Every couple of years, it seemed, he'd take it upon himself to stick his nose where it didn't belong, seizing on some feeble pretext to broach the subject of Culdee Creek and her family obligations. His unsolicited interference never failed to enrage Devra. What gave him the right to imagine he could interfere in family matters? Just because her father treated him like the son he'd never had didn't mean Ross was a MacKay. But he may as well have been, for all his strutting around the ranch like some banty rooster.

Devra's lips thinned into a tight little line. Well, he'd soon see things had changed. And if he didn't choose to change with them, he'd be out of a job. She had no time to waste and couldn't spare what little time she had on a man she all but despised.

After what seemed endlessly rolling hills, Ross finally turned right and headed east once more. The last of the forest faded away, and they were out on the open high plains. The sun glimmered behind a transparent coating of clouds, illuminating the faded grasses until they almost gleamed with a silvery hue. Scattered ponderosas now dotted the land. In the distance behind them, Pikes Peak, frosted with snow, loomed high and proud. And then, at long last, the furthermost barbed-wire fences of Culdee Creek came into view.

In spite of herself, Devra's heart quickened. She clenched her hands into tight fists, fighting the impulse to lean forward in anticipation of that first glimpse of the outbuildings and main house. Then they were there, topping one last hill to pass beneath the tall pine posts with the ranch's carved sign swaying languorously from its cross beam.

"It never changes, does it?" she forced herself to say with an edge of boredom. Somehow, her lack of enthusiasm for ranch life had always seemed to rankle Ross far more than it ever had her father. Knowing that, she loved playing the little game to its fullest. "No matter how many years pass, Culdee Creek is always there, same as ever, solid and dependable like some faithful old dog."

"I never quite saw this place in that light before," Ross said, guiding the truck down the hill toward the main house. "But then, some things *should* be solid and dependable. Home, family, God. In the end, they're really all we can ever count on in this life."

Devra shot him a sharp look. She had always managed to get a rise out of Ross with far greater ease than she was today. "You know, for someone so keen on home and family, I find it strange that you've never put yourself out much to acquire either of them for yourself."

"I didn't need to," he said as he pulled up before the main house. "Culdee Creek's always been home enough for me, and you, Logan, and the folks here have been family. Couple that with work I love and the Lord God above, and what more does any man need?"

"Not much else, I guess," she muttered, wondering at the same time who Ross thought he was fooling. "But then, some people are easily satisfied, or maybe just not that ambitious."

He switched off the ignition and turned to her. "Maybe so. But it's not really the time for us to pull off the gloves and go at it like we have in the past, is it? Later maybe, after your father's been prayed over and buried, and after we get things settled with Sam. Then maybe you and I need to have it out once and for all. But not now."

Ross extended his hand. "For Logan's sake, let's make peace, if only a temporary one, okay?"

She stared at his proffered hand, almost afraid to touch it. But he was right. What mattered just now was paying her father his proper respects, seeing to the ceremonies of death and burial, bringing the circle of one life, at least, to its completion. It wasn't about her. It wasn't about Ross. It was about Logan MacKay, her father.

Shame filled her, and, motivated by that realization,

she took Ross's hand and squeezed it briefly before withdrawing. "Okay, it's a deal. Peace it is, at least for the time being."

He grinned then, setting the gold flecks sparkling in his rich brown eyes. Once again, Devra's heart did a wild flip-flop. How could she have forgotten how beautiful his eyes were?

"Well, that's a relief." Ross pulled the key from the ignition, shoved it into his vest pocket, and opened the truck door. "Thelma just walked out onto the front porch. Why don't you two ladies get all that hugging and kissing out of the way, while I get your luggage and bring it inside?" As he opened the door, an icy blast of wind rushed in. "Looks like snow tonight. Glad you got here today, before the weather turned bad."

Devra climbed from the truck and looked toward the Front Range. Even now, thick clouds were slowly engulfing Pikes Peak. Soon, there'd be no mountains to see. Ross was right. Snow, and most likely some bitter weather, was on its way.

The prospect of bad weather didn't do much to lift Devra's already dismal frame of mind. If they got snowed in, there'd be no escape, no respite. Not from Ross. Not from the ranch. And not from the knowledge that she'd never see her father again.

Suddenly, Devra wished that she hadn't come home.

four

*A*rms outstretched, Thelma McCune hurried down
the covered front porch steps. A woman of mod-
erate build and ample bulk, she drew Devra in one of her
hugs that always made the younger woman feel as if she
were enveloped in some soft, comforting pillow. And the
emotional perception was equally as strong as the physical one. But then, she and Thelma went back a long while.

The older woman—who despite her sixty-plus years still
colored her thinning, overly permed hair in a shade that
could only be described as mandarin orange—had first

come to Culdee Creek the summer after Devra's mother's death. Still devastated by losing Anne MacKay to a drunken driver's carelessness three months earlier, Devra had readily turned to the compassionate, loving woman. Thelma had become her friend and confidante, her comfort when life turned harsh or confusing. And Thelma had always supported her in all her dreams and aspirations, even when Devra had met with gentle but firm parental opposition when she'd revealed that she wanted to become a doctor.

As she stood there, savoring the housekeeper's embrace, Devra's glance snagged on Ross, who, with an overloaded suitcase in each hand, was walking to the base of the porch steps. She still regretted that she had never shared her secret crush for the handsome drifter with Thelma. But Ross had arrived at Culdee Creek soon after Thelma, and Devra hadn't been ready to divulge her attraction for a grown man—and at twenty-one, Ross had definitely seemed a grown man—with anyone. If she had, maybe Thelma could've talked some sense into her and saved her from what ultimately became a humiliating and hurtful experience.

"It's s-so good to have you here, sweetie," Thelma said, her voice gone husky and unsteady. "Sure w-wish it was under better circumstances, th-though. I'm just so sorry. So sorry."

Devra pressed the older woman to her. "So am I, Thelma," she whispered. "What are we going to do without Daddy? Nothing'll ever be the same. Nothing."

The tenderhearted housekeeper began to sob then, clutching Devra tightly. "N-no, it won't. And, though I know the g-good Lord above will look out for us, it scares me, it does. Scares me and h-hurts. Oh, how it hurts!"

Devra almost regretted admitting her fears to Thelma, seeing how it set her off. But as a physician Devra knew that all their thoughts, as jumbled and painful as they might be, were but expressions of grief. Expressions better dealt with in the light of day rather than crammed down into some deep, dark corner of one's heart to eat away at one's soul.

"We're all scared and hurting." She slid an arm around Thelma's waist and gently turned her toward the front door. "But we'll get through this together. We still have each other, don't we? And we still have Culdee Creek too."

Thelma lifted a tear-streaked face. "Yes, you're right. We'll always have each other and Culdee Creek."

Devra wished she had bitten her tongue rather than utter that last bit about the ranch. She had meant only to offer comfort, but in doing so had seemingly committed to a course of action she had not yet given a thought to. Now, however, the realization that a lot of people's livelihoods were caught up in her decision about Culdee Creek struck her with a startling intensity. Nothing would be simple, it seemed.

As they walked into the house, Devra released Thelma and turned to hold the door open so Ross could enter with her luggage.

"I'll put your stuff up in your old bedroom for now, if that's all right with you?"

With his words, yet another fact assailed her. If she wanted to, she could now claim her father's bedroom as her own.

"That'll be fine." She forced a smile. "I think I'll be more comfortable there, at least for the time being."

Ross managed a bleak smile of his own. "I thought you might."

"I made up your bed with fresh sheets, aired out the room, and dusted and vacuumed everything this morning," Thelma piped up brightly as Ross left the living room and headed for the stairs. "Here, let me take your coat, and then let's go have us a nice hot cup of tea in the kitchen. I think it'll do us both a world of good."

At that particular moment, as she stood in the living room of her childhood, with the scent of a real Christmas tree filling her nostrils, Devra wanted nothing more than to run and hide in the privacy of her bedroom. But Ross was up there right now, and nothing was served by running and hiding anyway.

One way or another, death didn't let you hole up for long. And it seemed Thelma needed the comfort of a cup of tea and a return to the old routine of sharing it in the cozy kitchen. *"Just us two girls,"* Thelma had always liked to say as, with a conspiratorial giggle, she'd lean toward Devra from across the table and grin.

"Sure." Devra nodded and forced yet another smile. "A cup of tea would be wonderful."

The kitchen hadn't changed in years, not since her mother remodeled it shortly after Devra's birth to update it with the newest appliances available at the time. Of course, that made everything over thirty years old, and Devra couldn't help but think another remodeling was in order. As she looked around, her glance caught on the black cast-iron cookstove that had been around since the late 1800s. "Old Bess" remained as recalcitrant as it had been in those days. Luckily, it was rarely used now, save for the few times when the electricity went off in the winter.

In Devra's opinion, it was a definite antique—well, dinosaur, really—that had long ago outlived its usefulness. When it came to Old Bess, her parents had been far too sentimental, to the point of impracticality. With the next kitchen remodel, Old Bess was on her way out.

As if happy to be able to do something with herself, Thelma began to bustle around the kitchen. Soon, she had not only two rose-painted individual teapots sitting atop their own cups steeping tea on the table, but also had added a plate of chocolate chip cookies brimming with pecans and thick chunks of chocolate.

Devra eyed the cookies as the housekeeper finally took her seat at the table. "Those look sinfully fattening."

Thelma grinned. "Of course they do. That's what makes them taste so good."

41

Devra picked up her teapot and poured some of her favorite herbal tea. "Well, I think I'll pass on the cookies. I need to keep my girlish figure."

"You know as well as I that chocolate's a girl's best friend. Nothing improves the mood better than chocolate." Thelma placed two cookies on the plate set before Devra. "And if there are two girls more in need of better moods right now, I can't say as how I'd know them."

She had a point, Devra thought as she eyed the baked delights. And Thelma's cookies were absolutely scrumptious, made from prize-winning county fair recipes. She could almost taste that first bite of crispy cookie and rich chocolate melting on her tongue . . .

"Oh, you're right. Who cares about a few extra pounds at a time like this?" Devra picked up a cookie and bit into it with relish. "Ummm, these are *so* good," she finally said after polishing off the first cookie in three bites. She proceeded to consume a second cookie, then drain her cup of tea.

Thelma chuckled and shoved the plate heaped high with additional cookies toward her. "There's more where those two came from."

For the first time in the past day and a half, Devra's smile was genuine. "Two'll do me for right now, my dear. I don't need to stuff myself, you know."

"Well, I don't know about that." The housekeeper paused, then frowned. "Now, what kind of life have you been living there in New York anyway? I've been dying to ask you about that for the past three or four years now, but your father always told me to hush up about it, so I did. Now, though, I'm going to ask."

Devra poured herself another cup of tea, then looked up to meet the older woman's steady gaze. "I'm not sure what you're asking, Thelma. I mean, one minute we're talking about cookies, and the next . . . well, the next it seems the topic has suddenly changed to my life in New York. What exactly do you want to know?"

"Well, for one thing, are you happy there?" Thelma rested her forearms on the table and leaned toward her. "And is this doctoring you're doing with all those high society ladies really the path you want to take?"

Indignation filled Devra. Where did Thelma get off asking questions like that? Of course, she was happy. Of course, she was satisfied doing plastic surgery on rich women. Modern medicine wasn't intended only for the poor and destitute. And she took good care of her patients, made them happy. What more could anyone ask of a doctor?

True, she had deviated a bit from her original goal of becoming a facial deformity reconstructive plastic surgeon, specializing in birth defects, trauma, and burn victims. But there had been that huge medical school loan to pay off, not to mention her internship, residency, and initial office set-up costs. If she had taken on all those charity cases right off the bat, she knew she would've dug herself into a debt she might never have gotten out of.

43

Even with her lucrative and growing practice, she still had a few more years to go before all her loans were paid off. The sale of Culdee Creek would be the perfect solution to ending all her debts, but Devra didn't want to—indeed couldn't—deal with that sort of decision right now. Right now, it took all her powers of concentration just to focus on what she and Thelma were talking about.

"Yes, I'm happy with what I'm doing," she answered at last. "And I very much enjoy what I do. It's a good life."

Thelma looked down at her cup of tea. "So good you don't ever want to come back home to stay?"

She should've known this was where Thelma was leading. As supportive as the housekeeper had always been of her medical career, Thelma, like most people at a time like this, tended to cling to what was safe and familiar. And Devra couldn't really blame Thelma for wanting her to return to Culdee Creek permanently. She had to admit to a few twinges of yearning for the familiarity of home herself.

Still, nothing was served by giving the woman—or anyone else at Culdee Creek who might care—false hope that would only hurt the worse when it was finally dashed. Devra smiled gently and nodded.

"That's pretty much how it is, and has always been. I left Culdee Creek behind a long time ago and never looked back." She reached across the red-and-white-checked tablecloth and took Thelma's hand. "You understand that, don't you? You always did before."

The housekeeper's lips trembled, and fresh tears filled her eyes. "Well, before, your father was still alive, and a MacKay owned and worked Culdee Creek. But now he's gone. What'll become of the ranch if you don't come home and care for it?"

An edge of hysteria was beginning to tighten Thelma's voice. If she wasn't careful, Devra realized, the woman would soon be wailing at the top of her lungs, surely drawing Ross into the room and the discussion. And Ross Blackstone was the last person Devra wanted involved in this particular discussion at this particular moment.

She squeezed Thelma's hand. "I don't know. I don't have any answers right now. Please, Thelma. Daddy's not even in the ground yet, and I'm going to be here for the next couple of weeks. We've got plenty of time to talk about this later."

"Y-yes, I suppose you're right." The old woman swiped away her tears with the back of her hand. "I'm sorry. I'm just not thinking any too clearly, and when I first caught sight of you . . ."

"I know." Devra gave the old housekeeper's hand a final squeeze, then released it and leaned back. "I don't suppose any of us are thinking clearly right now."

She paused, took up her cup of tea, and drained its contents. Footsteps sounded across the living room's hardwood floor. The front door opened and closed.

Devra looked up. "Guess that was Ross. He's never been one for social niceties like saying good-bye, has he?"

"Oh, his manners are good enough. I think he figured he'd forced his presence on you enough for one day, that's all."

Devra sighed. Her and Ross's mutual antipathy had never been lost on Thelma. "Well, if it's any consolation, Ross and I have made a temporary truce."

Curiosity flared in the housekeeper's eyes. "Have you? Tell me more. Inquiring minds want to know."

Devra shrugged. "I've told you all there is to tell." She pushed back her chair and rose. That was all she needed right now—Thelma getting some wild ideas about her and Ross into that scheming head of hers. "Now, if you don't mind, I'm going upstairs to unpack and maybe even take a nap before supper. I didn't sleep well last night. I think jet lag is beginning to catch up with me."

"Yes, you do that, sweetie." As if her thoughts had already moved on to something far more important, Thelma absently waved her off as she stirred another spoonful of sugar into her tea. "You have a nice nap, and I'll fetch you when supper's ready. Yes, that's a very good plan. Go take a nap."

five

*H*er room was just as she had left it the last time she had come home. The double bed with its red, white, and blue handmade log-cabin quilt, matching quilted pillow shams, and contrasting ruffled blue gingham bed skirt. The old wooden rocking chair that had been refurbished countless times over the many years of its existence, and was now lightly stained and varnished to bring out its original oak grain. An antique sewing machine sitting on a small table, and a worn doctor's bag that held a place of honor on her bookshelf. The lace curtains at her window that, as Devra looked through them, framed a scene of thick, white flakes against a backdrop of opaque gray sky.

Everything looked so familiar and at the same time so foreign. Not that she hadn't experienced the sensation for a while now, really since she had first left home to attend medical school, heading out East like her great-great-aunt Beth had, to become a doctor. The old saying that you couldn't go home again was so true. Or at least that you couldn't see things with the same eyes.

This time, though, everything had taken on an even stranger appearance. Everything had a raw edge, like a dressing that had been ripped off a wound, leaving it bleeding and painful. Bleeding, painful, and yet something more. Something that went far deeper, hinting at a great sorrow, a devastating loss.

A loss of innocence? A loss of trust in the safe certainty of life and one's ability to exert any real control over it? Devra's mouth quirked sardonically. *After all you've seen in your years of medical training and practice, you'd think you would've learned that by now.*

But it was different seeing life's tragedies played out in other people's lives. You could distance yourself from those. Indeed, as a physician, you *had* to or risk being dragged down into other people's grief and confusion, leaving you to be of no help to anyone.

But Devra knew that standing on the outside looking

in at other people's lives also insulated you in a cocoon of false security, lending an equally false sense of control over your own destiny. It made you feel invulnerable, as if all the truly bad things happened to other people and always would.

Devra closed the door to her room. Her two big suitcases had been placed before the closet. Briefly, she considered unpacking them and putting all her things away. But then a bone-draining weariness overwhelmed her.

There was enough time to deal with that chore later. Thelma was right. She needed a nap.

She kicked off her Italian leather boots, shed her cobalt blue cashmere wool jacket, and headed toward the rocking chair where a crocheted afghan lay draped over one arm. Picking up the blanket, Devra made her way to the bed. She climbed up, settled herself on the pillows, then pulled the afghan over her.

Instead of the blessed respite of sleep, however, memories—in rapid succession—assailed her. Memories of warm summer days, of riding the rolling hills of Culdee Creek with her father, of the tall grass shimmering silver and green beneath the caress of a gentle breeze. Memories of bright, crisp autumn days, as she and her father made their annual drive up the tortuous curves of Ute Pass and into the mountains to see the aspens turn their glinting gold and orange colors against the contrasting backdrop of deep-green pines. And then there were the memories of Christmases past.

Even that first year after his wife's death, Logan MacKay, with the good-hearted Thelma's assistance, had resolutely kept to all the traditional MacKay holiday customs. They had trudged endlessly, or so it had seemed to Devra, around Culdee Creek until they found the perfect Christmas tree. They had joined the Yule log hunt held every year in one of the nearby towns. They had attended the annual Nutcracker Suite ballet. And, of course, they had decorated the Christmas tree, wrapped presents, made the requisite amount of cookies, and attended Christmas Eve services at St. Michael's.

They'd had to drive to Colorado Springs for church, as had all the MacKays since Grand View's demise. Not that it mattered much, with the increasing amount of paved roads and faster cars over the years. More and more business was transacted in the ever-growing Colorado Springs, and a twenty- to thirty-minute drive would get you almost anywhere in town anyway. Get you to where the real conveniences were, the things that really mattered.

Her father hadn't seen things quite the way she did, though. He deplored the ever-quickening pace of life. The growing need for multitasking. The emphasis on the bottom line over people in the endless search to squeeze out just one more cent. The impersonality of businesses and how they treated their workers, with the resultant lack of loyalty and pride in one's work.

Though her father had some valid points, Devra couldn't

help but consider a lot of his views as those of a man who, over the years, had fallen behind the times. Efficiency was of the highest importance these days. So many of the inventions, like cell phones and pagers, were vital in serving others all the better.

Which reminds me . . . Devra thought as she climbed from bed to walk to the dresser where she had left her purse. It was past time to switch on her cell phone, now that she was off the plane and back home. Susan had to be able to reach her in case of emergencies or questions she couldn't easily answer.

Devra paused and looked down at the little black phone in her hand. Who was she kidding? She wasn't as vital as she liked to believe. After all, there were two other physicians who had offered to take any calls while she was gone. But she had refused, just as she had always done in the years past.

Guilt tugged at her as she remembered last Christmas Eve. Her cell phone had begun ringing in the middle of services at St. Michael's. One of her former patients had called from some party, wanting her to talk with her best friend and a prospective client.

The woman's questions had gone on and on, and Devra had all but missed the rest of the service. Though Ross and Thelma had glared at her when she returned to her seat, her father hadn't said one word or acted as if anything out of the ordinary had happened. Which was true, Devra realized sadly. She had made it clear for several years where her priorities lay.

She walked back and sat down on the edge of the bed. "I'm sorry, Daddy," she whispered. "I didn't mean to be inconsiderate. I just thought . . . I just thought I was putting my patients first."

I know, sweetheart. She could almost hear her father's reply, recalling the nearly identical conversation they'd had last Christmas. *It's just that you have things a bit skewed. Put God first, then your family and self. Only then will you have the abundance to give back to others as they deserve. Otherwise, you drain yourself so dry that what little you retain for yourself is of small value.*

Even now, similar tears of frustration filled her eyes. "That's not true," Devra had said in her defense. "I've always tried my best. I've always thought of others over myself. Just because I don't share your religious beliefs anymore doesn't mean I'm not a good, giving person!"

The memory of the look of reproach he had sent her made her heart ache. *I never said you aren't a good, giving person, sweetheart. You're just an incomplete one, and you can only give from your incompleteness.*

It was hard to argue against such reasoning, especially when it came from her father, who knew her better than anyone. Not that she hadn't tried time and again, bound and determined to prove him wrong. But she had never won, though her father finally had conceded that she had the right to live her life as she wished. She'd never won because, deep down, she knew that at least some of what he had said was true.

She had always imagined that someday they'd work through that debate to each of their satisfaction. Maybe when she was a bit older and more experienced, she would've come to understand him better. Maybe when her currently hectic pace slowed a bit, she would've had the leisure to spend some intensive time at Culdee Creek, searching out the mysteries of life that still eluded her, guided by her father's wise and able hand.

But now that chance was lost.

"Oh, Daddy, Daddy," Devra sobbed, clasping her arms around her. "Why did you have to die? Why? I still need you. There's still so much we have left to say to each other. And now . . . now who will I talk to? Where will I go?"

No reply came this time, neither in her head nor from her memories of all the conversations they'd had over the years. There was nothing but a sense of isolation—and an anguish so deep and devastating she thought she might die.

She was alone. The two most important people in her life were gone now, and she wasn't ready for it.

It wasn't fair. And ultimately, there was only one Person to blame.

"I hate You, God," Devra muttered through tears that now ran hot and angry as she bent over and rocked herself to and fro. "Do You hear me? I *hate* You!"

six

*S*now fell all night and the next day. By the following
morning, a thick blanket of white coated everything.
The sky, however, showed no signs of letting up on its generous outpouring of the fluffy white stuff. By 9:00 A.M.,
when Devra was set to leave for her father's funeral, the
snow had accumulated an additional four inches, reach-
ing three feet or more where the wind had caused drifts to
pile up. But thanks to Ross's and several of the other ranch
hands' four-wheel-drive vehicles, everyone was still able to
make it to town in time, where they were joined by the

MacKay kin who lived locally, as well as those who had gathered from other parts of the country.

At the church, Devra's actions were almost robotic—greeting the mourners as they arrived, going through the motions of the funeral service, and accepting additional condolences at the luncheon reception hosted by the ladies of the church. She was amazed at how little sleep a person could get and still function. Just smile, nod, murmur a few words of thanks as you shook yet another person's hand. *Yes, Daddy will be missed. Yes, he was a wonderful man. Please, help yourself to a plate of food. Thank you so much for coming.*

Afterwards, Devra, all her relatives, and the Culdee Creek ranch family headed back home by way of Grand View's cemetery, where Logan was interred next to his wife in the large MacKay family plot. When the priest had finished blessing and praying over the casket, he lingered for a moment more to speak with the various mourners. Soon, though, the bitter winds and below-freezing temperatures began to drive everyone back to the relative warmth of their cars.

Joseph MacKay, Logan's younger brother, made his way to where Devra stood gazing down at the open grave. "Everyone's meeting up back at the ranch." His glance locked with Devra's as she dragged it up to meet his. "You're not going to stand out here too long, are you? It's pretty miserable, and you can always come back another day when the temperature's more tolerable."

Devra smiled weakly. Her uncle looked so much like her father. "I won't be much longer, Uncle Joe. Just make yourself at home. I'm sure Thelma'll have something warm to drink waiting for you."

He nodded, his mouth twitching into his own imitation of a smile. "Knowing Thelma, I'm sure she will." Joe reached out and gave her arm a quick squeeze. "I'll keep everyone entertained until you get there."

She watched him turn and walk past Sam Dillon, who must've been standing back, waiting for his turn to speak with her. Swallowing down a weary sigh, she smiled once more, this time in greeting.

"Thank you again for coming, Sam." Devra extended her hand to him as he drew up before her. "It's such a comfort, knowing how many people loved my father."

"Yes, I'm sure it is," the tall, silver-haired man said. "Logan's passing . . . well, it's going to leave a big hole in a lot of people's hearts." He paused, glanced around at the rapidly thinning crowd. "The weather reports for the next few days aren't real promising. I'm thinking we might all be snowed in soon. And since I came down from Denver for the funeral, and our appointment to read your father's will was for tomorrow anyway, I was wondering if we might just all head back to Culdee Creek, get together in your dad's study, and finish this? If you think you're up to it, of course."

She wasn't up to anything right now, but she also knew

that feeling wasn't going to improve any time soon. "Might as well get it over with, if Ross is willing."

"He is. I already asked him, while you were busy saying your good-byes to everyone. In fact, he's heading back to Culdee Creek to get everything and everyone settled, in case you were willing to have the will read today."

Devra looked around and caught sight of Ross's big pickup pulling out through the cemetery's tall, wrought-iron gate. Irritation flashed through her. Was it just her imagination, or was Culdee Creek's foreman a bit overeager?

She shrugged off that unkind thought. Whatever Ross Blackstone's motives, the sooner they had this unpleasant business over with, the better. Besides, with the way she was feeling right now, there wasn't much in any will that could make her feel worse.

"Sure." Devra nodded. "No sense dragging this out. The snow doesn't look like it'll ease up any time soon. It's better not to risk any unnecessary trips—especially all the way to Denver—for the next few days." She paused and glanced around. "I guess I'm going to need to bum a ride off of you, though. Ross was my last chance for a ride back to the ranch."

Sam grinned. "Oh, we took that into consideration." He turned and gestured gallantly toward his maroon Land Rover. "My chariot awaits, m'lady."

From the corner of her vision, Devra saw the cemetery staff, two locals with shovels in their hands, edge discreetly forward. She looked back at the open grave where her father's remains were now laid. Already, almost a half inch of snow covered the casket. It almost looked as if a soft, white blanket shrouded the plain but elegant box. *Oh, Daddy, Daddy.* She closed her eyes for a moment. *I know you're with Jesus in heaven now, but why did you have to leave me so soon? Jesus has plenty of friends up there with Him, but I only have you.* She winced. *I only had you.*

"It's getting cold out here." Devra opened her eyes to meet Sam's compassionate gaze. "Let's get going and let these poor men finish their work. There'll be plenty of time for me to come back later."

The old lawyer nodded and offered her his arm. "Yes. Plenty of time."

seven

"his shouldn't take long," Sam said as he laid the second copy of the will before Devra and handed the third one to Ross, who sat at the other end of the expansive brown desk. "It's pretty simple and straightforward, just like Logan was." He pulled his own copy closer, lifted the cover page, and looked first to Devra, then Ross. "Why don't we all take a few minutes to read before we get down to discussing this?"

Devra's glance skittered off the cover page, which boldly proclaimed this to be the last will and testament of Logan

MacKay. Her stomach clenched tightly. She had seen the same scene enacted in so many movies that a strange sense of déjà vu engulfed her. It was almost as if . . . as if she were playing some part now. Or maybe it was just some unpleasant dream she'd soon wake up from. Oh, if only it were just some dream!

Once again, numbness settled over her. She embraced it as the blessing it was.

"Sure," she said, her own voice sounding strangely hollow as she lifted the cover page. "Let's just take a few minutes to read."

"My beloved daughter . . ." Devra's gaze skimmed the expected words that commenced her father's will. *"My dear and cherished friend, Ross Blackstone . . . I leave all my possessions, including the ownership of Culdee Creek Ranch, to Devra MacKay . . ."*

For the first time since she had begun reading the will, Devra dragged in a breath. Okay, no surprises here. Just the normal wording.

Her breath caught in mid-exhalation. *". . . one condition to fulfill in order for my daughter to gain ownership of Culdee Creek . . ."* Her gaze jolted to a stop. *"She must agree to take up permanent, full-time residence on the ranch. If she refuses, I leave title and ownership of Culdee Creek Ranch to Ross Blackstone . . ."*

A crazed mix of emotions assaulted Devra. Shock, disbelief, then a raging flood of indignation and anger.

She jerked up her gaze to meet Sam's. "This is outrageous! First, that my father should set such terms. Second, with all the MacKay relatives still alive and willing to take over Culdee Creek, that my father would ever, *ever* put Ross Blackstone in such an advantageous position. It's obvious that Mr. Blackstone must've somehow manipulated my father. I mean, my father was ill, and Ross could've taken advantage of his frail condition, in order to gain such an unbelievable status in the will."

She whirled around to glare at Ross. "There are legal recourses to such devious, underhanded actions, you know, and you've picked the wrong person to try to pull this on. I, of all people, know the kind of man you really are, Ross Blackstone!"

Ross neither flinched nor averted his gaze. "I didn't take advantage of Logan, Devra. And the issue of what would happen to Culdee Creek when Logan died never came up between us, save that he once bemoaned the fact that you didn't seem interested in the ranch. But that was it, Devra. I'm as surprised about this as you are."

"But you're not interested in opting out of the will's conditions, are you?" she all but snarled. "On the contrary, I can see the dollar signs bright and clear in your eyes."

"Logan wanted you to have the ranch, Devra. That's apparent enough in the will." Though something akin to anger flared in his eyes, Ross's tone of voice remained soft and controlled. "And the only dollar signs you might be seeing are because I hope you'll decide to keep me on as foreman. Culdee Creek's my life, my home. All I want is to stay and help run the ranch."

"Fat chance of that now!" Even as the sense that a trap was closing in on her filled Devra with panic, fury consumed her. "This little ploy of yours has put an end to any hope of us ever working together. If for no other reason than to see you gone, I'll keep Culdee Creek!"

At the realization of what she had just said, her mouth clamped shut. The situation was impossible. She'd have to give up her practice, her life in New York, all her plans. Her hopes and dreams would disappear. And her father . . . her father would finally have his way.

Frustrated tears filled her eyes. Furiously, she blinked them back. She turned to Sam.

"You're the lawyer. What can I do to get this will changed?"

"Considering I was the one who helped Logan write up this will, and he was definitely of sound mind at the time," the older man replied, "not a whole lot, I'm afraid. Just because you're not happy with the terms doesn't mean it isn't legal or won't stand up in a court of law. And it isn't as if your father isn't offering to leave the ranch and everything else to you, Devra. It's not like you're being cut out of the will."

He shoved back his chair and shot an impassive look at Ross before swinging around to impale Devra with one of his lawyerly stares. "And might I also mention the fact that it wouldn't be the smartest move in the world to get rid of Ross? What do you really know about running a ranch the size of Culdee Creek?"

This was getting her nowhere. Devra sent the dark-haired foreman one final, scathing glare. Though she still had half a mind to fire him on the spot and send him packing in the middle of this miserable snowstorm, caution finally prevailed.

Sam was right. Ross was now the primary set of brains, and a lot of the brawn, behind Culdee Creek. As much as she hated to admit it, she desperately needed his knowledge and assistance. It would be stupid to fire him just now, and she wasn't a stupid woman.

"Fine," she muttered. "Your point is well taken." She turned to Ross and forced herself to tamp down the rage she still felt. "I apologize for my earlier harsh words. As you might imagine, I'm not in the most objective frame of mind right now. I'd appreciate it if you'd stay on and help me with the ranch, until I can deal with things more dispassionately."

He studied her for a long, tension-laden moment. "I'll stay for as long as you want me to, Devra," he replied finally. "I owe Logan at least that much."

But not me, she thought. *If it'd just been for me, you'd hightail it out of here in a heartbeat, wouldn't you? Well, I'm no fool, Ross Blackstone. You don't trust me any more than I trust you. And just as soon as I can manage it, you're history.*

She pushed back her chair, picked up her copy of the will, and stood. "Well, this is just about all I can stomach for one day. I'd appreciate it if we keep the terms of this will private for the time being. And in the meanwhile," she added, glancing out the window at the falling snow before looking down at Sam, "you'd better head on back to Denver while you still can. I doubt the roads are going to be passable much longer."

"Yeah, I suppose that'd be a good idea." The older man climbed to his feet. "If there's anything else I can do to answer further questions when you've had time to process it all, give me a call, Devra. Though I've a legal responsibility to see the terms of your father's will carried out, I also want to support you in making the decision that's best for you." He smiled at her. "Never doubt that for a minute."

She gazed up at him, and instead of emotion, all she could feel was emptiness. All she wanted to do was trudge upstairs to her room, crawl in bed, and pull the covers over her head—to shut out the world and pretend that none of this had ever happened.

But she couldn't. Suddenly, all choice had been taken from her. And she didn't like what remained. Didn't like it at all.

eight

With her head splitting and her mouth dry clear down to her vocal cords, Devra awoke late the next morning. She lay there for a while, staring up at the ceiling fan, feeling anguished and overwhelmed. It seemed the dawn of a new day had done nothing to put a fresher, more positive perspective on things.

She had two men to thank for that. Her father for dying and putting that ridiculous clause into his will, and Ross Blackstone for . . . for just being Ross Blackstone. Now that she considered it, that conniving fraud had probably been planning to get his hands on Culdee Creek from the very first day he had walked on the ranch. His ultimate intent had been there in everything he had done, from acting like the loyal, hardworking ranch hand and then foreman, down to his finally "finding the Lord" and joining the same church the MacKays attended.

With a snort of disgust, Devra rolled over and bunched her pillow beneath her head. She should've seen it all a long time ago, but she had been too busy with her own life to notice the subtleties playing beneath the surface. And once she had left home for good, there was no one left who was as wise to Ross as she had been. No one had remained to protect her father, who Devra knew had missed her terribly and so was vulnerable to the ploys of a man who had immediately stepped in to assume the role of a son.

At the admission, guilt trickled in to fill the gaping wound left by her father's death. She had to bear some of the blame, she supposed. If she hadn't been so caught up in her own life, her own needs. . . . But it wasn't as if she hadn't always loved her father and wanted the best for him. She had just wanted the best for herself too.

The fragrant aroma of freshly brewed coffee and some sort of baked good wafted up from the kitchen. Devra smiled. If she didn't miss her guess, Thelma had a big sheet of her famous sticky buns just about ready to come out of the oven.

She flung back the covers, climbed from bed, and donned

her robe and slippers. No sense wasting the day hiding up in her bedroom, she decided as she headed out the door and down the hall to the bathroom. Besides, she needed a good jolt of caffeine, as well as the sugary, high-calorie nutrition of a couple of sticky buns, to clear her head and fuel her body for the day's battle.

Ross Blackstone needed to be set straight on a few things, before the issue of the will got too far out of hand.

Devra paused at the kitchen doorway to run a quick hand through her hair to ease out any tangles. Then she headed straight to the cupboard to get down a big pottery mug and immediately filled it with coffee. At her entry, Thelma, a pan of sticky buns in her hand, closed the oven door and turned to her.

"'Bout time you were up and at 'em, Miss Sleepyhead." She laid the pan on the stove, picked up a plate and spatula, and began transferring the buns to the plate. "I know the past few days have been hard on you, but no good is served by hiding away in your room, either."

Thelma laid the towering pile of sticky buns in front of Devra, who had taken a seat at the kitchen table. "Here. Have a few. It'll help sweeten your disposition, which, I can tell by that sour expression on your face, is in dire need of some improving."

Devra shot her an exaggerated grimace, then took a sticky bun. With barely a pause, she bit into it, savoring the pecans, the rich caramel syrup, and the tender, yeasty bun. "Ummm," she murmured before washing down the first bite with a swig of coffee. "You know these are the real reason I come home every year like clockwork, don't you?"

The housekeeper laughed. "Good. I can still expect to see you once a year then, can I?" Her smile faded. "Now that your daddy's gone, I mean. Aside from my Johnny, you're just about all the family I've left in this world."

Thelma's words about her ailing husband jolted Devra back to the reality of things. She motioned to the chair across from her.

"Have a seat. I need to tell you about the fine pickle Daddy left me in."

"You're talking about the will, aren't you?" Thelma walked to the cupboard, took down a mug, and poured herself some coffee before returning to the table. "I figured something was up last night when Ross hightailed it out of here, and you stormed upstairs to your room just as soon as you said your good-byes to everyone." She leaned forward, cradling her mug between her hands. "What was in the will that upset the both of you, sweetie? And how can I help?"

Devra sighed. If only Thelma *could* help. "I'm afraid this is between Ross and me. Daddy left the ranch to me if and only if I agree to come home for good and run it. If I don't, Culdee Creek goes to Ross."

"*What?*" The housekeeper's eyes widened. "Culdee Creek in the hands of someone besides a MacKay? Why, that's unheard of! And that's no offense to Ross, mind you, but whatever was your father thinking . . ." Her voice faded as a light of understanding brightened her eyes. "I knew Logan was desperate to get you back home by hook or by crook," she said, "but I never thought he'd go this far." She shook her head. "Oh, Logan, Logan. This isn't fair. It just isn't fair."

Fresh anger filled Devra. "No, it's not fair, but I'm not so certain Daddy was in his right mind when he made out that will. I'm not so certain it was really his idea. I'm sure it was someone else's. Someone who stood to gain it all if I was pushed out of the way."

"I don't understand, sweetie." Confusion momentarily clouded Thelma's eyes before comprehension seemed to dawn. "You can't mean . . . you surely aren't accusing Ross of taking advantage of your father?" Vehemently, she shook her head. "No. I won't believe that. Ross wouldn't do such a thing."

"And why not?" Devra couldn't keep the rancor from creeping into her voice. "We all know how much he loves Culdee Creek. I mean, the man lives and breathes it. If he's got any kind of an outside life, I sure haven't seen it. And knowing how I've always felt about him, he probably figured I'd fire him just as soon as Daddy was gone. So what did he have to lose, and he sure had a lot to gain, in working Daddy bit by bit to put him in the will? It's the only explanation for all of this."

"Maybe." Thelma shrugged. "But have you ever once given any thought to the possibility that your daddy was just desperate to get you back home where you belong, and away from the temptations and empty promises of the life you're leading now? Have you?"

Devra couldn't believe what she was hearing—and from Thelma, her biggest supporter, no less! "For one thing," she ground out, "I'm not leading a life of temptation and empty promises. And another thing, why the sudden 180-degree turn? Of all people, I thought you understood me and my dreams."

"It's precisely because I *do* understand you and your dreams that I'm now saying what I'm saying." The older woman leaned back in her chair and exhaled a deep, weary breath. "You've lost your way, sweetie. The life you've made for yourself in the big city isn't the life you'd originally planned, nor is it any sort of life that'll win you eternal happiness."

"Oh, so it's back to the religion thing, is it?" Devra gave a strident laugh. "Well, I'll have you know it's entirely possible to be a successful businessperson and still get to heaven. In fact, it's pretty narrow-minded of you to pass judgment on me."

"Every way of a man is right in his own eyes: but the Lord pondereth the hearts." Thelma steadily met her gaze. "That's from Proverbs, you know."

"That has nothing to do with you turning on me like this!"

"Yes." The housekeeper nodded with a firm emphasis. "Yes, it does. I have to tell you the truth, sweetie. Always have and always will."

There was no talking Thelma out of something once she got her mind set on it. Besides, Devra reassured herself, in the end it didn't matter what Thelma thought anyway. When it came to her own life, what mattered was what *she* thought.

With the half-eaten sticky bun still languishing on her plate, Devra pushed back her chair and rose. "Well, all I can say is that God may know what's in my heart, but you certainly don't. And as long as you insist on taking Daddy and Ross's side, you'll never understand me."

"So what are you going to do now?"

"What else?" Devra snapped. "Since I've started the day fighting with you, I might as well make the misery complete by chasing down Ross and having it out with him too. Then, for the next week or so until it's time for me to head back to 'Sin City,' I'll avoid you all either by spending plenty of time in town or hiding out in my room!"

73

nine

*S*he knew she had acted rather childishly back there with Thelma, Devra thought as she trudged through the thigh-deep snow toward the first two of the barns. But she couldn't help it. Thelma's betrayal had hurt. Hurt deeply.

Had almost everyone at Culdee Creek turned against her? Ross's antagonism she could understand. They had never gotten along. But Daddy and Thelma?

A stiff wind blew past, and with a shiver she hunkered down deeper into her father's well-worn, hooded down jacket. In her hurry to get to Colorado Springs, Devra hadn't paid much attention to packing, which resulted in too many expensive wool suits and silk blouses and not enough practical winter clothes. She was lucky she had, at the last minute, thrown in a couple pairs of jeans, three pullover sweaters, and a handful of pairs of warm socks. Devra supposed she could get along well enough with those things combined with the old hiking boots and a pair of knit mittens she had left behind in her bedroom closet. After all, it wasn't as if high fashion was expected or even practical most times on a ranch.

Her glance lifted to the leaden sky. The clouds were so thick that not a ray of sunlight could pierce them. It was an altogether gloomy day, but at least the snow had stopped. When the four walls of country isolation began to close in on her—which Devra knew they would in another day or so—she could at least commandeer one of the ranch trucks and find some respite and desperately needed mental stimulation in town. Though Colorado Springs most certainly wasn't New York City, even a few hours spent at one of the quaint coffee shops that had sprung up all over town would be treat enough after the inevitable boredom of Culdee Creek.

At long last, Devra reached the first barn. A quick perusal of its cavernous interior and a good whiff of horse manure later, she ascertained no one was around. Five minutes later, she entered the second barn. Two hands were busy repairing a stall partition.

Devra walked over. "What happened?"

With his hammer, Chuck Mahoney pointed in the direction of a gray horse ensconced in another stall down the way. "Old Duke there got it into his head to try and pay a visit to one of the mares. When Ross and I tried to stop him, he threw the poor guy clear through this stall. Kind of tore up Ross's side a bit, so I sent him up to his house to doctor it while Mike and I put the finishing touches on Duke's stall." He arched a shaggy gray brow. "You being a doctor and all, Miss Devra, maybe you could pay Ross a house call and check him out. He sure looked in some pain when he left."

Though she doubted Ross would be in the mood for any of her particular plastic surgery skills, it might be the perfect opportunity to get the upper hand. If he was in pain, he surely wouldn't be thinking clearly. She might be able to trick him into admitting the part he played in orchestrating her father's will. It was certainly worth a try.

"Sure. I'd be glad to see how he's doing." Devra smiled. "I take it Ross still lives in the house up by the pines?"

Chuck nodded. "Yep. You betcha."

Devra turned and left the barn. Ten minutes later, her breath coming in short, shallow gasps, she arrived at Ross's front door. When several knocks received no response, she began to get worried. As much as she disliked the man, Devra really didn't care to find him dead in a pool of blood. Problem was, if he was already unconscious, he wasn't going to make it to the door anytime soon.

She opened the front door and stuck in her head. "Ross? Are you all right?"

When no answer was forthcoming, Devra entered and closed the door behind her. "Ross?"

A low groan emanated from the kitchen. Her pulse quickening, she hurried across the small living room to the closed kitchen door. Without thinking, she walked in to find Ross standing there bare-chested, a long gash running nearly the length of his right side.

At the sound of her entrance, he wheeled around. Shock registered in his eyes. "What are you doing here?"

Devra wasn't sure if he was angry or just surprised. Either way, it didn't matter.

"Are you all right? Chuck and Mike told me you'd been hurt, and then I heard you groan . . ."

Ross gave a disgusted snort and indicated his shirt. "I groaned because this was my favorite shirt, and now it's ruined. I'm never going to forgive that horse, not if I live to be a hundred!"

Typical macho man. Well, she had dealt with her share of those types in her years at Culdee Creek, not to mention medical school and her internship. Besides, it was so typical of Ross to keep his true feelings shut away.

"You'd better let me have a look at that." Devra gestured to the raw, angry wound in his side. "It looks pretty nasty."

His mouth quirked with wry humor. "Nasty, huh? That doesn't sound very medical to me. Where did you say you went to school?"

Devra rolled her eyes. "The New England School of Quack Medicine, of course." She walked over and indicated the kitchen table. "Hop up on that, young man," she said, donning her most professional physician's manner. "Let's have a look at you."

Hesitation glimmered briefly in his eyes, and for a second Devra thought he might refuse. Then with a sigh Ross climbed up on the table, lifted his right arm out of the way, and presented his side to her.

On closer examination, the gash wasn't as bad as she had first imagined. True, the skin surrounding the actual wound was badly bruised and abraded, but the open area was less than a quarter of an inch deep. It was, however, raw, red, and oozing.

"You should head into town and get this cleaned and sutured at the ER," she said, finally glancing up to meet his gaze. "A tetanus booster and some antibiotics might be in order too, considering where you got this injury."

"My shots are all up to date, and I'm not one for pills, so I'll hold on the antibiotics for now. And why do I need to go all the way to town when I've got a doctor right here who can clean it?"

She looked him in the eye. "I hate to disillusion you, but we doctors don't carry our medical bags with us anymore. And I plumb forgot to pack the sutures and needles."

"Well, I don't intend to have a piddling little thing like this sutured anyway. One more scar among many sure isn't going to matter at this point in my life." Ross inclined his head to a big red plastic toolbox that sat on the kitchen counter. "There are plenty of first-aid supplies in there, including steri-strips. You can use them, if you want to."

"Suit yourself. It's your hide, after all."

Devra retrieved the first-aid box, set it on the other end of the table, and began sorting through it. It was a well-stocked kit, she had to admit, with plenty of gloves, gauze, ABD pads, cling bandage for wrapping wounds, irrigation syringes, bottles of sterile saline, and tubes of antibiotic ointments. There was also a generous assortment of varying sizes of steri-strips.

She glanced up. "There's nothing in here for pain, and I assure you it's going to hurt like the devil when I start cleaning it. You've got some splinters scattered in among all the torn-up flesh, you know." Devra arched a brow. "Any whiskey available? That always seemed to work in the good old days."

Ross chuckled and shook his head. "Nope, not anymore. Gave that up, along with my wild ways, when I turned to God."

"Well, then you'd better offer up a quick prayer for some

pain relief," she muttered as she began to dig into the first-aid box and pull out all the necessary supplies. "Because you're going to need it." Triumph filled her as she found what she had been looking for—a pair of narrow-tipped surgical pickups. "Great! This'll make all the difference."

"A pair of tweezers?" He frowned. "Well, I see you're easily pleased. Except when it comes to God and me, anyway." Ross lowered his arm and, gripping the table edge, leaned toward her. "Why's that, blue eyes?"

She shot him a digusted look and laughed as she donned a pair of gloves. "Oh, come on, Ross. Don't pretend you don't know why I don't like you. And just a word to the wise. This isn't the best time to open up that particular can of worms, at least not when I'm getting ready to poke and prod at your side."

He smiled. "Well, then, why don't you like God anymore? When I first came to Culdee Creek, you were such a devout, God-loving girl. But over the years, after you left home for college and medical school, you seemed to pull away from going to church and praying."

Devra snapped open a 100-cc bottle of sterile saline, took out a sterile syringe, and filled the syringe with saline. "Not that it's any of your business, but I still believe in God. And I try to live a good life, treating people with kindness and honesty." She turned and thrust a handful of dish towels at him. "Which is more than I can say for the likes of you."

"And what am I supposed to do with these? Stuff them in my mouth?"

"I like the sound of that," Devra said. "But first, just hold a couple down below the wound. It'll catch the irrigating fluid that'll escape when I flush it. And you're more than welcome to stuff them in your mouth when I'm done."

Ross gave a snort of laughter, then did as she suggested. The first syringe of saline was delivered with a bit more force than necessary, if the big foreman's sudden intake of breath was any indication. But better, Devra rationalized, to make sure the wound was flushed as well as possible. In the end, it'd save him the worse pain of removing whatever splinters the flushing didn't take care of.

He bore the repeated irrigations without complaint. Finally, though, Devra was ready to debride the wound of remaining splinters and any ruined flesh. "Can you lie down on the table with your side up now? It'll make it easier to see what I'm doing."

"Sure." Ross lowered himself to the table, then drew up his legs. "Just tell me what you need."

What she needed was for him not to lie there looking so attractive. He had always been a fit man, leanly muscled, broad-shouldered, and trim of hip and legs. But she had never seen him less than fully clothed, even in the hottest weather. And if his hair-roughened upper torso wasn't disconcerting enough, the scars on his chest and arms certainly gave her pause. On closer inspection, they looked like bullet and knife wounds. How and when had he gotten them?

She had never heard much about Ross's life before he had come to Culdee Creek. When she'd asked him about his past, shortly after he'd arrived at the ranch, he had bluntly told her it was none of her business. And her father had quickly changed the subject when she had tried to pry any information from him. But that had been long ago, when she was still a girl. Would Ross tell her now if she asked?

"You were right about one more scar not mattering." She pretended an intense concentration on the task at hand. "Are you ever going to tell me how you got them?"

He hissed in pain as she snipped a little too closely to live flesh while cutting away the dead skin.

"Sorry." She met his gaze. "Got a bit too enthusiastic there."

"It's okay." Ross managed a taut smile. "Do what you've got to do."

"So, was that your way of changing the subject, instead of taking the chance of making your surgeon mad?"

For an instant, he looked puzzled. "Oh, you mean your question about my scars. No, I wasn't trying to change the subject. I was just wondering if it would be wise to tell you about my sordid past, considering your already dismal opinion of me. How I got the scars, I mean."

"Well, considering my already dismal opinion of you can't get much worse, I can't see that it'd do much harm." Once more, her gaze lowered to her work. "So why not try me?"

"Okay. The bullet holes are from robbing a bank when I was seventeen. The knife wounds I got from a prison fight, trying to protect myself and my cellmate. Fortunately, I survived my wounds. My cellmate didn't."

Her head snapped up. "You were in prison?"

He met her stunned gaze with a calm one of his own. "Yes, for four years. I was only an accomplice and not the ring leader, but I was still tried as an adult. My older brother got ten years." His mouth twisted. "Not that he had a chance to live long enough to do his time."

Devra laid aside the tweezers and scissors. "What happened to him?"

"He was my cellmate. Being the hothead he was, he managed to make some of the other prison inmates mad. Guys who pretty much ran the inside show. They came for him one night. I tried to help fight them off, but we were unarmed and they weren't. I was lucky. They only cut me up. But they killed my brother."

Ross had been twenty-one when he had first come to Culdee Creek. It didn't take a rocket scientist to deduce that he had come here straight from prison.

"Did . . . did Daddy know you were an ex-con?"

"Yeah. I told him up front. I'd already made enough mistakes to fill a lifetime. I didn't want to make any more."

"Oh. I see." She quickly approximated the wound edges and applied steri-strips, then opened some sterile 4x4s and covered the wound with them and two ABD pads. Next, after peeling off her gloves, Devra opened the cling bandage package and began to unroll it. "Here, lift up a bit so I can get this underneath you. I want to wrap the dressings over your wound with this to hold them in place."

Ross complied, and she was soon securing the cling bandage with several pieces of tape. "All done," she said. "I'll stop by tomorrow to check you and change the dressings. And no more work for the next few days, or you really will be making a trip to the ER."

Ross chuckled. "Yes, ma'am."

Devra turned back to the task of cleaning up the mess she had made.

"So was it a mistake then?"

She looked up. "What?"

"Was it a mistake telling you about my past? Does it give even more credence to your already low opinion of me?" He shrugged. "I mean, makes it even more plausible now, doesn't it, that an ex-con would scheme against you to steal the ranch?"

He should've stopped while he was ahead. Devra's simmering anger at him exploded once more. "Yes, I suppose you could say that. I mean, isn't there some saying about 'once a thief, always a thief'? And that's exactly what it'd be if you got your hands on Culdee Creek. You're not a MacKay and never will be, no matter how hard you tried to cozy up to my father all those years." She gave a harsh, unsteady laugh. "You'd have been smarter, if Culdee Creek *was* what you've always wanted, to have cozied up to me when you had the chance. Then sooner or later, you would've had Culdee Creek through me."

"Yes, maybe I could have," he replied quietly, his dark eyes searing a path clear to her heart. "But I wouldn't ever marry a woman just to get her ranch. And especially not you, Devra MacKay."

ten

I wouldn't ever marry a woman just to get her ranch.
And especially not you, Devra MacKay."

She lay there in the soft, gentle darkness that was her
bedroom for a long while that night, turning Ross's words
over and over in her mind. Try as she might, she couldn't
make sense of what he had said or, more to the point, what
his true motives had been in saying it.

Why especially not her? Because he despised her so
much? Because if he were the last man alive and she the
last woman, he'd never want her for his wife?

Devra groaned and buried her face in her pillow. Well, what had she expected from him after all these years? That he'd suddenly open his eyes and see her for the attractive, successful woman she was? Fat chance of that! Odds were, the only sort of woman who would ever attract Ross Blackstone would be some prim and proper, holier-than-thou little church mouse. She'd have to be meek and mild at the very least, and consider him the finest man who had ever walked the face of the earth—with the exception of Jesus, of course.

No, she definitely wasn't Ross Blackstone's kind of woman. He had made that painfully clear a long while ago. Thinking back now to that humiliating moment, Devra couldn't recall ever seeing such a look of horror on a man's face. Then, to add insult to injury, he had compounded the terrible hurt by opening his mouth and speaking.

"Why are you doing this to me?" he had demanded in outrage. *"Everything I have is tied up in this ranch—my hopes and dreams, my future—and you, because you feel a need to try out your newly discovered wiles on the first available guy, haven't given the potential consequences a second thought. Well, you've chosen the wrong man. I don't have time for little girls."*

She had tried to proclaim her innocence, that she wasn't toying with him, that she loved him. Loved him from the first moment she had set eyes on him, and would love no other for the rest of her life.

But Ross Blackstone hadn't believed her. He had just

shuddered in revulsion, then turned and walked away, not caring about the heart he had left broken and bleeding in the dirt. And for a long while after that humiliating day, in the times he couldn't manage to avoid her, he had borne her presence with the long-suffering demeanor of a man forced to endure the most tiresome of children.

That's all she had ever been to him—a tiresome child not worthy of his time. Even now, there were still moments when she suspected he barely tolerated her—if the hasty retreats he soon made whenever they happened to end up alone were any indication. And, much to her chagrin, his cruelty still continued to hurt her.

It was that aspect of coming home every year that unsettled her most of all. That Ross would always be there and that sooner or later, no matter the defenses she threw up to protect her heart from him, he'd hurt her again. Devra thought she hated him most of all for that.

But he wouldn't hurt her this time. Not this time and never again, she told herself as she flung herself over and stared unseeing into the blackness. This time she'd seize the upper hand. This time, she'd take control, stand up for herself, and make Ross Blackstone admit she was a person—a woman—worthy of respect.

It wasn't all she wanted. But it would have to be enough.

The next morning, one day before Christmas Eve, Devra awoke to a wonderful gift—a break in the gloomy and unseasonably cold weather. Sunlight streamed in, illuminating the insulated blinds until the window coverings glowed golden. She leapt from bed, ran to the window, and pulled the cord to lift the shades.

The first thing she saw was white. A white that was both blinding and sparkling at the same time. The dark green of the ponderosa pines, with the rich, red-brown bark of their sturdy tree trunks, contrasted perfectly, as did the deep, cloud-strewn blue of the sky.

This was the Colorado winter she knew—glinting, sun-kissed, and pristine, with postcard views that stretched on in all directions. Devra smiled wryly. A far cry from New York winters, which could be charming in their own way, though the snow didn't stay clean for long and the tall barricade of buildings hindered any possibility of scenic vistas.

Simplicity and a slower pace versus the potential for endless excitement and opportunities. That summed up the difference between life at Culdee Creek and life in one of the biggest and most exciting cities on earth. And maybe that summed up the reason for her conflicted emotions as well. How could she choose between the two when she wanted both?

At least in New York, she had kept far too busy even to recognize the problem, much less deal with it. With a pensive sigh, Devra let the window blind fall back in place and headed for the bathroom.

A half hour later, after a leisurely soak in the tub, Devra dressed in one of her loose chenille sweaters and a pair of jeans and loafers. She ambled into a kitchen filled with scents of frying bacon, hot, rich coffee, and toast. Thelma was carefully ladling two perfectly poached eggs onto a plate already garnished with three strips of bacon and one lightly buttered piece of toast.

"Here, eat up. We have to be at church in an hour and a half. With the snow-packed roads, we'll need to allow some extra time."

Devra accepted the plate but not the ultimatum. "I think I'll stay behind. I don't go to church much anymore."

The housekeeper's brows came to a perfect point. "And since when did this begin? You've always gone to church with us in the past."

"Well, that was just to please Daddy." She smiled apologetically. "But I guess I should tell you that I haven't attended church in about five years. Except for Christmas Eve services, I mean," she hastened to add, noting the frown forming on Thelma's forehead. "It just wouldn't be Christmas without all the carols, and the reading of the Christmas story, and the nativity scene, and all the other decorations."

The older woman made a disgusted sound and stalked back to the stove, where she poured out a steaming mug of coffee. "If you don't carry Christ in your heart all year round," she proclaimed as she set the coffee before Devra, "there's little sense pretending for a couple of days a year. Is that how it is for you now, sweetie? Have you turned away from our blessed Lord and Savior?"

Suddenly, the plate of food didn't look all that appetizing. With great difficulty, Devra bit back a swell of anger. Everyone, it seemed, was pressing in on her to conform to their expectations, from her father, who even posthumously sought to coerce her into coming home, to Ross, who always seemed to imply that she wasn't good enough, to now even Thelma, who appeared intent on haranguing her into going to church and giving her life back over to God. Well, she was who she was, and if none of them could accept that, then that was their problem, not hers.

"I've had just about all the pricking and prodding I can handle." Devra pushed back her chair and got to her feet. "I'm sorry I'm such a disappointment to you and Daddy, but I like myself and the life I've chosen just fine, thank you very much! And I'm not going to be browbeaten or made to feel guilty because I'm not living up to your expectations. Either accept me as I am, or I'm done with all of you for good. Do you hear me? For good!"

As she glared down at Thelma, tears filled her eyes. The realization angered her all the more. She didn't cry. She just didn't! Yet in only a few days spent back home, all her carefully acquired control had disintegrated and flown to the four winds.

Maybe she shouldn't be surprised, Devra admitted. After

all, she had just lost her father. And grief did strange things to people. She just hadn't anticipated how strongly *everything* would affect her, or how totally chaotic her life would suddenly become.

It seemed home wasn't a safe place anymore. It seemed Culdee Creek was too full of painful memories and unrequited dreams. And it seemed like nothing she had formerly believed in now made any sense.

"Sweetie, I'm sorry." Thelma extended a hand to her, her gaze compassionate and concerned. "I didn't mean—"

"No." Devra began to back away. "Don't add lying on top of everything else. You and I both know exactly what you meant. And the truth is, I *have* turned from God. There's no room in my life for Him anymore."

She turned then and fled to her bedroom, where she remained until she heard Thelma and Ross climb into his pickup and drive away.

eleven

*I*t was midafternoon before Devra left her bedroom. She knew she owed Thelma an apology. She just didn't feel quite up to it yet. Her heart was still too raw.

When she had received the news of her father's death and set out on the journey home, she had thought that the difficulties of dealing with that loss and the admission of life's unpredictability would be burden enough. But now she realized that grief and loss were multilayered things. So many issues—some of which she now knew had been unresolved and shoved into some corner to be dealt with "later"—had a strong impact on how she coped with such a soul-shattering wound.

She had never come to any peace with her father over her unwillingness to return home and join him in running Culdee Creek. Because of that, there had always been that tiny bit of mutual disappointment—he for his only child who could not follow his dreams by following in his footsteps, and she for the parent who could not seem to accept her for what she had become. She had imagined, however, that the love between them had been strong enough to overcome that.

Her mouth went tight. *Well,* Devra quickly amended, *strong enough until I read the terms of his will.*

She had also imagined Thelma's love to be sacrosanct and even more unconditional than her father's had been. But now, today, she realized she had been wrong about that too. Thelma wanted her here at Culdee Creek as much as her father had. And Thelma wanted her to turn back to God as well.

God . . .

Devra sighed and shook her head. There was always that niggling guilt overshadowing everything else. What Thelma had put into words a few hours ago had lingered at the edge of Devra's consciousness for a long while. God *had* been shoved aside, to be brought out when she finally found the time to deal with Him. Next year maybe, when things slowed down, when she had more time.

God didn't need her, after all, and her patients did. God would understand.

As she headed down the stairs, Devra gave a sharp little laugh. Just about the only thing that hadn't changed since she had returned to Culdee Creek was her relationship with Ross. Almost as soon as they had seen each other, the barely contained antagonism had flared to life. And, true to form, Ross had quickly fanned the flames to even greater heights, in what appeared to be his overt manipulation of her father's will.

Maybe that was why she was actually looking forward to her next meeting with the foreman. She knew he and Thelma were back from church. She had heard his pickup stop outside the house to deposit Thelma before heading up the hill to his place. Rather than deal with the house-keeper just yet, Devra decided to get Ross's dressing changed. She secretly hoped for some freshened anger to set her troubled mind in order.

He was out on his front porch, sweeping away some lin-gering snow. Devra frowned as she walked up the porch steps.

"I thought I told you no work for the next couple of days."

"Yeah, I know." Ross grinned sheepishly. "But it was such a tiny bit of work, and I'm trying not to use that side at all."

Devra grabbed the broom from him. "Sit." She indi-cated the wrought-iron and cedar bench that abutted the house wall. "Since you seem to be unable to ignore any kind of work that needs doing, I'll finish this for you."

"That's not necessary, Devra. I—"

"Sit, I said. Doctor's orders." Devra began sweeping the porch with long, back-and-forth strokes. "In case you haven't figured it out yet, for the time being at least, I need you to run this ranch. And you need to stay in good shape to do that."

"For the time being, is it?" Ross took his seat on the bench and leaned back. His mouth quirked. "So, have you made up your mind then to stay on at Culdee Creek?"

Her cheeks flushed hot. Most likely from the sudden exertion, Devra chose to tell herself. Or maybe, instead, from the anger that never failed to rise whenever she was long in his presence. Either way, it felt good.

"No, I haven't." She didn't care to meet his gaze, so she kept sweeping away. "But one way or another, you know as well as I that you're now the man with all the knowledge about this ranch. And since neither one of us wants Culdee Creek to run into any problems during this time of transition . . ."

He gave a sharp bark of laughter. "You know, Devra, one of the many things I've admired about you was the way you always got straight to the point. You never leave me wondering for long what's really on your mind."

She paused in her sweeping to look up then, meeting his smiling gaze with a scorching one of her own. "I think we stopped pussyfooting around each other a long time ago. And since we've also given up any pretense of liking each other, it makes things so much easier, doesn't it?"

His smile faded. "I never said I didn't like you, Devra."

For a moment, she didn't know what to say. Was the man insane, or just lying to try and lull her into a false sense of security? Well, it didn't matter. Not anymore.

"Yeah, right, Ross." Devra herded the last pile of snow across the porch and swept it through the railing. "Save the charm for someone who doesn't know you and might believe it. You don't need to start flattering me to keep your job. You've already got it for as long as I need you."

"And how long might that be? Should I be typing up my resume anytime soon?"

Exasperation filled her. "Look, I only found out about the will two days ago. Cool it on the resume for a while, will you?"

He cocked his head. "Fine, but are you sure you can trust me in the meanwhile? Not to sabotage you or anything, I mean?"

His question took her aback. *Did* she trust him? Well, that was ridiculous! Of course, she didn't trust him! She had never trusted him, or at least not since he'd broken her heart. But that was a different sort of trust than trusting him to take care of Culdee Creek. If nothing else, Ross Blackstone had always taken care of Culdee Creek. Even Devra could see that.

"When it comes to you and me," she said, "I trust you about as far as I can throw you. But I know you won't do anything to hurt Culdee Creek." She smiled thinly. "After all, you're still hoping to get your hands on it. And you've never been the sort of man who'd cut off his nose to spite his face."

"Not usually," he muttered grimly. "But there was that one time . . ."

"Well," she said, setting the broom aside, "I want to go to town today, and I need to see to your wound and dressing change first, so let's get that taken care of, okay?"

"Sure." He rose to his feet, turned, and headed to the front door. "Been looking forward to it all day, especially with the memory of your gentle hands on me the first time. Dreamed about it all night even."

Devra almost ran into him as he paused to open the door. Her glance traveled up his six foot and then some length. She laughed.

"Yeah, I can just imagine what you dreamed about, and it was probably nightmarish, considering how painful debriding a wound without even any topical anesthesia is. It'll be better today, though, I promise. Nothing worse than ripping off a dressing that has probably dried onto the wound anyways."

He arched a dark brow. "Really, is that all? Piece of cake."

She gave him a shove, suddenly aware she was actually enjoying their verbal give and take. "Well, we'll see. I make no promises. I'll just forewarn you that your dressing change isn't the wisest time to aggravate me in any way."

"I'll be the soul of proper decorum," Ross said as he opened the door and motioned her in. "You can count on me, ma'am."

Devra watched Ross remove his shirt, lay it aside, and climb onto the kitchen table to once again facilitate her inspection and care of his wound. She found it strange that it was even harder today than it had been yesterday to contemplate touching him, much less getting as close as she needed to do a proper job. It was almost as if, at least when it came to Ross, all her hard-won professionalism went flying out the window. There was a lot to be said for the common physician practice of never treating one's family and close friends. She had just never had to face that reality before.

Not that Ross would ever be considered either family or a close friend, Devra hastened to assure herself. He'd hurt her again in a heartbeat if she lowered her guard long enough to give him the opportunity. She had only to remind herself of the fiasco that was her father's will, thanks to Ross Blackstone's meddling.

"Something wrong with the dressing?"

The object of her contemplation's amused voice interrupted Devra's thoughts. She looked up.

"What?"

Ross chuckled. "I was just wondering if there was something wrong with the dressing, considering how hard you were staring at it."

Warmth flooded her face. That was the second time he had made her blush today, and she hadn't even spent fifteen minutes in his presence. Her behavior was beginning to border on the ridiculous.

"I was just considering my options," she replied brightly, purposely pulling her lips into what she hoped was some semblance of an evil grin. "Rip off your dressing in one fell swoop or pull it away slowly and painfully."

"More like *savoring* your options," he muttered with a shudder. "But you're the doctor. Whatever you do, I'm sure it'll be in my best interest."

"Oh, great. Put the guilt trip on me." She expelled a mock sigh of disappointment. "You patients always know how to get everything your way, don't you?"

Devra moved close, removed the tape holding the cling bandage in place, and began unrolling it from around his torso. Thanks to the gauze and thick ABD dressings covering his wound, nothing had leaked through to stain the cling bandage. At least she'd be able to reuse it.

Next, she removed the ABD pad and gently peeled away the gauze dressings. Surprisingly, the wound drainage had been minimal. There was no inflammation, and the steristrips were still holding the wound edges together well.

"Well, that didn't hurt half as bad as I thought it might." Devra tossed the soiled dressing into the trash can, removed her gloves, and added them to the trash. "If I'd really ripped off your dressing, I risked pulling off most of your steri-strips too. I only suggested that option to scare you a little." She grinned. "It does my heart good to see a big man like you quiver a bit from time to time."

"All big men, or just one in particular?" Ross asked, grinning back at her.

She stroked her chin, pretending to consider that for a moment. "Hmmm, now that you ask, just you, I think."

"And did you enjoy yourself?"

"Well, a little more moaning and groaning would've helped."

They both laughed then, and Devra was struck with the realization that she had never spent so much time talking to Ross as she had in the past days since her return home. Or felt so relaxed, so carefree, so . . . happy being with him. How was it, after all these years of hostility, they could now stand together and laugh—and her father was barely cold in the ground?

Remorse washed over her, followed by the realization that she didn't know whether to blame herself or Ross. Her head lowered in shame. *Oh, Daddy, I'm so sorry. I don't know what's gotten into me, but please forgive me. Please.*

"Devra, what's wrong?"

Once again Ross's deep voice pierced the clamor of Devra's thoughts. She jerked up her head and began to open several packages of gauze sponges.

"N-nothing. Nothing's wrong. I just need to get this done, that's all. I've got errands to run."

He grabbed her hands, stilling them. "No. It's something else." His rich brown eyes gleamed with concern. "All of a sudden, everything changed. You remembered something. What was it?"

His voice was so gentle, so caring. She almost told him, almost broke down and wept. But the long years of keeping her emotions in check served her well. And there was the innate caution she had learned to have around him as well, instilled by equally long years of coldness and rejection. It rose now to shield her in an impregnable suit of armor. A suit of armor she desperately needed at this particular moment, lest she break down, throw herself into Ross's arms, and surrender what little dignity remained in her.

"I remembered that we're not friends, and never can be," she said, hating herself for the icy edge to her voice but just as desperately needing the coldness rushing through her veins to bring her back to reality. "In fact, in my saner moments, I don't even like you."

As she spoke, Devra slowly but inexorably dragged her hands from his gently confining grip. "You've been a user of people, especially my father, for a long while now, but not anymore. The will was the last straw. The game's up, Ross. The source of endless cash to feather your nest has run dry."

twelve

For several tension-laden seconds, Ross didn't say anything. He didn't even look at her, averting his gaze to stare down at the floor while he gripped the table edge. Devra knew that this time, her words had finally cut hard and deep.

He had gone pale. The long, angular line of his jaw had tensed, and his mouth drew into a tight, thin line. Muscles bulged in his arms, as if he fought to keep them at his side.

In all the years she had known him, Devra could count

on one hand the times she had ruffled Ross's composure, much less angered him. She had managed to do both this time, though.

Strangely, the victory wasn't as sweet as she had always thought it would be. As the seconds dragged on, she began even to regret her harsh words. Why was it Ross always brought out the worst in her?

"Why did you call me that? A user of people, I mean?" He glanced up, impaling her with a steely gaze. "What have I ever done—aside from my supposed manipulation of your father to change his will—to feather my nest here at Culdee Creek?"

And where should she begin? There were so many things she had kept firmly tamped down all these years, because she felt like her father sometimes favored Ross over her. The fact that her father had adamantly refused to listen each time she had tried to convince him his foreman wasn't the fine, upstanding man he thought he was, however, had hurt the most. It was almost as if . . . as if Logan MacKay had chosen to take Ross Blackstone's word over hers.

"I don't see any point in going over all the schemes you've hatched," Devra muttered. "It won't change anything."

He slid off the table and came to stand before her. "What schemes, Devra? Name me one. Just one."

Okay, she thought. *So he wants to play that game, does he?* "Well, let's see." Melodramatically, she scratched her head. "Could it be . . . could it be how you conned my father into paying for your entire college education?"

The look of incredulity on Ross's face would've almost been comical if the topic of conversation hadn't been so serious. Devra, however, was hardly in the mood for laughter.

"Paid for my college? Whatever gave you the impression—" Ross halted in midsentence. "Oh, the loan. You thought when Logan gave me the up-front money to get my animal husbandry degree at CSU, that it was a gift rather than a loan. Well, it took me a while after I graduated to repay him the full amount, but I finally did it, with interest."

Devra gave a disbelieving snort. "Easy to say, since the only other person involved in the transaction is dead."

Ross sighed and shook his head. "So now, on top of everything else, you're calling me a liar? You know, Devra, you really need to stop while you're ahead."

"Is that a threat, Ross?" She stretched to her fullest height of five feet six.

"No," he replied, his eyes gone dark with . . . what? Pity? Sadness? "It's just a warning that you're getting ready to make a fool of yourself."

"Well, you're hardly the man to do it!"

"Aren't I?" He all but bit out the words as he wheeled around and stalked to the small desk shoved in one corner. After jerking open several drawers and riffling through the papers and folders there, he appeared to find what he was looking for. He grabbed up a thick manila folder, then turned and strode back to her.

"Here. These are the transcripts of all the classes I took at CSU, and the bills for those classes. There are also detailed records of each and every payment I made to your father to reimburse him, *with* interest, down to the last penny." He all but shoved the folder in Devra's face. "Take a look. See what you think."

She eyed the sheaf of papers protruding from the folder. "That doesn't mean anything. Those are your files, not my father's."

His gaze narrowed. "Your father signed off on each and every payment I made him. And I have receipts for all my checks."

This was beginning to get out of hand. Devra cursed her unkind tongue.

"Afraid to know the truth, are you?"

She had never been able to handle being challenged by Ross very well, and this time was no exception. Devra snatched the folder from his hand. "Fine. Have it your way, then." She stepped around him, laid the folder on the table, and opened it.

He had spoken the truth when he claimed to have kept detailed records. And there were plenty of receipts, stapled to copies of checks made out to Logan MacKay. All the receipts bore her father's distinctive signature.

Devra pulled up a chair and systematically began to

match receipts with every bill from CSU. It was hard to concentrate on the task with Ross standing nearby watching her, still disconcertingly bare of chest. But Devra's powers of concentration had been honed in far more stressful arenas than this. Besides, she wouldn't be surprised if Ross was gambling on the fact she didn't possess the patience to see this task through to its end.

Not that Ross'd had anything to risk, Devra finally admitted ten minutes later as she lifted her gaze from the last sheet and closed the folder. He had indeed paid back every cent her father had loaned him, with interest.

"I apologize," she said, her words simple but sincere. "I was wrong."

His expression was inscrutable. "And does that admission open up the possibility that you might be wrong about other things? Or do you just figure I won this round, and with a little more digging you'll uncover all the dirt you need on me?"

Through the muddy haze of her shame, a strange thought pierced her mind. Why would he possibly care *what* she thought, after how she had just treated him? If the tables had been turned . . .

But Ross was different from most other people, her included. No matter the anger, the accusations she threw his way, he kept on trying. He kept on turning the other cheek in the hopes that . . . that what? What exactly did he want from her? To grind her down until she didn't have any fight left? Or was it something else? Something kinder, more caring? More loving?

Was this man truly attempting to live the life of a follower of Christ? Her father had tried numerous times to convince her that his foreman was a good, decent man. Had he been correct all along?

Devra wasn't sure she cared to accept that premise. After all, it only made her pale in comparison once more, and she was tired of always paling in comparison to the apparently shining example that was Ross Blackstone.

But she was also beginning to get tired of all the battling between them—battling, she admitted reluctantly, almost exclusively originating from her side. What had it ever gotten her but added bitterness in her life, not to mention strained relations with her father? Maybe her father *had* known Ross better than she.

"Yes, maybe I was wrong about some things," she said. "And the things I wasn't wrong about happened a long time ago and don't matter anymore anyway. But I'm not just going to hand over Culdee Creek to you, Ross. It's MacKay land and holdings. One way or another, it's going to stay that way."

The merest vestige of a smile glimmered on his lips. "And that's where I want it to stay. In *your* hands, Devra."

She gave a sharp little laugh. "Well, I don't know if it's going to stay in my hands. The terms of Daddy's will are just too restrictive for that."

"If I'd known Logan was going to write it that way, I would've done my utmost to change his mind." He gazed down at her with a solemn intensity. "You've got to believe me about that. I would've tried my best. As much as I loved and respected Logan, he'd no right to box you in like that."

The old frustration swelled anew. "Then why did he, Ross?"

He shrugged. "I can't say for sure." He gestured to his right side. "Do you think you can finish up on this? I mean, now that we're back to being civil to each other again, it should be safe to let you near me, shouldn't it?"

She chuckled and shook her head. "Yes, it's quite safe. And it wasn't as if it wasn't great eye candy leaving you to prance around the kitchen shirtless for a while. I know plenty of women who'd have paid good money for the chance to see that."

For the first time in eons, Ross blushed. "Uh, should I take that as a compliment, or what? I never know with you."

As she finished opening the gauze sponges and some ABD pads, Devra threw back her head and laughed. "Oh, sure. Why not? After how I've been treating you lately, I suppose I owe you that and more." She motioned for him to climb back on the table and lie down. "Besides, just because I don't like you doesn't mean I haven't noticed you're a good-looking man."

Ross cocked his head. "Hmmm. You aren't flirting with

me, are you? I was thinking of offering to drive you to town to do that shopping, then maybe catch some supper before we headed home, but only if you're not flirting with me."

At that particular moment, Devra was grateful her head was lowered as she applied the dressings and began to wrap the cling bandage around Ross's middle to secure them. If not, she didn't know what her expression would've revealed. Most likely confusion, fear, and maybe even some crazy, if swiftly quashed, flare of hope.

But she couldn't pretend she hadn't heard him. Had he asked her out on a date? Or was he just attempting to cement what seemed to be their first baby step toward what might someday become a friendship? And even more importantly, did she want—did she dare—risk a friendship with him?

In less than a week since she had been back home, their relationship had taken several wild swings. The anger and bitter comments were standard. The common level of coolness in all their interactions was completely normal, even expected. But this playful bantering and the fleeting moments of honesty, not to mention Ross's seeming attempts to change not only the direction but the tenor of their interactions, was even more upsetting than their arguments had ever been.

No harm, though, in letting Ross accompany her to town, or in getting a quick bite. Actually, it was almost worth the startled reactions they'd get from Thelma and the hands who might see them drive off together.

"You can set your fears to rest," Devra said as she finished taping the end of the cling bandage in place, then handed him his shirt. "I'm not flirting. It wouldn't be professional of me to act like that with my patients."

Ross accepted his shirt and shrugged into it. "Good. Then it's a go for town and supper?"

"Sure." Devra grinned and nodded. "Considering where we've been, what do we have to lose?"

"Exactly," he replied with an equally resolute nod. "What do we have to lose?"

thirteen

"Thelma, I need to apologize for yesterday," Devra said late the next morning—Christmas Eve morning—as she stood in the kitchen doorway. "I blew everything you said out of proportion." She forced a wan little smile. "Guess I'm not handling Daddy's death quite as well as I might wish."

The housekeeper looked up from the bowl of sugar cookie dough she was mixing. She smiled in gentle understanding and nodded. "None of us are, sweetie. We just all choose different ways to show it."

Devra walked into the kitchen, a kitchen that smelled of comforting scents of baking cookies and brewing coffee. She glanced around. Thelma must have gotten up extra early to drive in from town and get this much baking done already. Every bit of flat surface in the room was covered with clean, brown paper bags and a mind-boggling assortment of treats.

There were gingerbread boys and girls, coconut and pecan topped cookie bars, bright red-and-green candy cane cookies, thumbprint cookies filled with jelly, two pans of rich, dark fudge, and a cookie sheet of cooling, crunchy peanut brittle. Across the room, on top of a nonfunctioning Old Bess, sat two apple, two pumpkin, and one pecan pie. Another traditional Christmas Day feast for all the ranch employees was evidently in the offing.

"Well, one way or another," Devra said, "just because I'm hurting is no reason to take out my pain on those I love. I guess the terms of Daddy's will are really getting to me more than I thought. I feel like he's trying to control my life and change me, even from the grave."

"And I made you feel that way too, didn't I, when I started in on you about God?" Thelma began to scoop big spoonfuls of sugar cookie dough into a cookie press. "I didn't mean to seem to judge you, sweetie. I just love our Lord so much and know what a comfort He is in times like these. But I won't harp on you anymore about religion, if you don't want me to."

Devra walked to the cupboard, took down a mug, and poured herself some coffee. "Well, if you could maybe leave it be for right now, that'd be a big relief. I know I've left God out of my life for a while now, and I'm not sure how to let Him back in. Maybe you *can* help me with that, but just not now. I'll go to Christmas Eve services tonight and all, though, because that's a MacKay tradition. But I just need some time to do some hard thinking. About God, about Daddy and the will, and—"

"About Ross Blackstone?"

The spoon Devra was holding almost followed the sugar into her mug of coffee. Her head jerked up, and she stared at the other woman.

"What in the world are you talking about?" she all but sputtered. "Ross has nothing—absolutely nothing!—to do with my current state of mind."

Thelma shot her a sly look before turning back to the cookie press. One by one, she pushed perfect little green Christmas tree shapes out onto the cookie sheet.

"Maybe not," she said with a shrug, never lifting her gaze, "but everyone's been talking about your daily visits to Ross's house, and that you both left yesterday afternoon and didn't get back until 8:00 or 9:00 last night. Talk has it you two are getting pretty chummy. If so, it's about time, I say."

Devra had forgotten how close-knit the Culdee Creek folk were, and how fast anything of interest sped through the ranch rumor mill. But her and Ross Blackstone? That was the most ridiculous thing she had ever heard!

"I was visiting him to take care of his wound, and nothing more." Devra made a soft sound of disgust. "And maybe we are beginning to get along a bit better, but no one needs to be starting any gossip about it."

"So, have you two at least worked out some sort of compromise? When it comes to the will, I mean?"

Devra was acutely aware that Thelma's attention had now turned completely from the cookies to her. Exasperation filled her. It seemed there was nothing about her life that wasn't under scrutiny, leastwise not while she was at Culdee Creek. For the first time in the past few days, she yearned for the anonymity of the big city.

"No, we haven't worked out any compromise. The terms of Daddy's will don't allow for any compromise from anyone. It's either I get the ranch or Ross does. And that's it, pure and simple."

"Oh, I don't know about that." Once more, the housekeeper turned to pressing out perfect little Christmas tree cookies. "I can see a lot of possible solutions, like you're still single, Ross has never married. And if I recall, you were once pretty sweet on him."

Devra could feel her cheeks growing hot. *"Once,* Thelma. That's the operant word. *Once."*

"It's never too late, sweetie." The older woman paused to remove the Christmas tree disk from the now-empty

118

cookie press, and replaced it with a round wreath one. "Maybe it's time to grab what's been there waiting for you all along. Ross. The proper stewardship of your God-given gifts. Your ties to Culdee Creek. Reclaim them before it's too late, before the time passes and they can never be regained.

"The Lord won't wait forever, if you insist on squandering what He's given you. Far better He look with favor on you, proclaiming 'Well done, my good and faithful servant,' than be thrown into darkness where there'll be weeping and gnashing of teeth."

Devra rolled her eyes. *"Really*, Thelma. Ross and Culdee Creek are hardly gifts. More like millstones around my neck. And I *am* trying to be a proper steward of my medical career. I work very hard. I mean, it's rare if I even have free time for myself. Everything I do is for others—"

"There are two temptations"—the housekeeper chose that moment to cut in—"and both of them are a misuse of God's good gifts to us. We can do nothing, or we can try to do everything, and so not do anything well. We can keep so busy that we avoid facing the truth about ourselves and our lives."

"And how, pray tell, is doing everything a misuse of God's gifts?" Devra asked, her irritation rising. "Because I know that's exactly the category you've placed me in."

"Your medical practice isn't the only gift God has given you, sweetie." Thelma smiled sadly. "He not only gives, but He wants for you to give *and* receive as well. To have balance in your life, simplicity, fullness, and time for Him. And He wants you to value and enjoy home and family too. It's why He brought you back here in this difficult time. To reexamine your life and priorities."

"And it took something as heartbreaking and life-shattering as Daddy's death to force me to do this? Is that it?"

"Maybe. Or maybe it was just time for you to open your eyes to your true obligations. Because the time is now, and you are here."

"And exactly what does that mean?" The sudden turn of the conversation was beginning to make Devra uncomfortable. She had already asked Thelma not to broach the subject of God, and here she was going at it again.

Thelma smiled and laid aside the cookie press. "Let me tell you a little story. It'll illustrate the point I'm trying to make far better than any long, boring explanation from me."

"A story, huh? I'm all ears."

Devra couldn't have asked for a better escape route than that. A story sure beat having to endure another lecture about God. It was also relatively safe. Stories were always open to personal interpretation. No one was necessarily right or wrong.

"Okay, then, here goes," Thelma replied with a chuckle. "Seems that some time during World War II a German lady hid Jewish refugees in her own home. Eventually some of her friends found out and, understandably, were very scared for her. 'You're risking your life,' they told her. 'Yes, I'm well aware of that,' she said. 'Then why are you doing this? Why do you persist in such insanity?'"

Thelma met Devra's puzzled gaze. "Do you know what that German lady said?"

Devra smiled and shook her head. "No, but I'm sure you're going to tell me."

"Yes." The housekeeper nodded. "Yes, I am. The German lady's answer was simple. 'I am doing it because the time is now, and I am here.'"

fourteen

ecause the time is now, and I am here . . ."

That afternoon, as the clouds rolled in, the wind began to blow, and the snow began falling again, Devra repeatedly turned the inspiring but disturbing little tale around in her mind. She had imagined stories to be safe and open to diverse interpretations, but she now began to realize how easily a story could lead one into a room of many mirrors.

Mirrors that, no matter which way she turned, reflected

her own life and beliefs, her hopes and dreams. Mirrors that, for the most part, didn't portray her in a flattering light.

But was that reflection really shining forth from her own heart or was it instead a compilation of everyone else's desires for her? Undoubtedly, since she had returned home, the clamor of requests had intensified, led by the demands both inherent and evident in her father's will. Considering the resultant high emotions, it was an easy enough thing to confuse the whisperings of her conscience with the demands emanating from others. Demands that she change her life, her relationship with God. That she come home for good.

Maybe that was why the story of the German lady resonated so strongly within Devra. She sensed that the verbal pushing and prodding of others would've never struck so close to home if she hadn't already been thinking the same things herself. What if Thelma was right? What if the time to face what she had and hadn't done with her life was now? What if she lost the chance? And what if it really *was* the hand of God pushing and prodding her to make proper use of her gifts?

After a time, Devra's pensive thoughts began to press on her so hard and insistently that she felt as though she were trapped in some prison. Despite the weather, she bundled up in a thick sweater and her father's down jacket, and headed out for a long, bracing walk. The cold was like a slap in the face, the knee-deep drifts a physical challenge to tackle, but Devra kept slogging on to the thick forest of pines up the hill and a special spot she hadn't visited in years.

The creek that ran through the ranch, bordering it on the south and east before spilling into a large pond, exited from the ponderosa pine–studded hills to the north of the ranch proper. Devra had always loved that area of the creek. Surrounded by tall, dense trees, it was a safe hiding place she had fled to many times as a girl—until the day her mother had died. Then she had stopped going there.

It had been too painful, after all, knowing how deeply her mother had loved the beautiful bridge spanning the creek. A bridge her father had built for his wife on their tenth wedding anniversary.

Her mother had always had a fascination with Asian—and particularly Japanese—culture. Far Eastern history and civilizations had been her favorite subjects in college. Well aware of his wife's interest, Logan had decided to surprise her with the gift of a curved wooden footbridge over one of the widest parts of the creek, high up in the pines. He had worked on the little bridge for weeks, painstakingly fashioning the intricate curves and railings, the arching, rounded floor, before finally painting it a glorious shade of scarlet.

Even now, as Devra drew up at the edge of the winter-sluggish, half-frozen creek, she could imagine her mother's joy when first seeing the bridge. The sight of the thin curved railings and the floor now covered in several inches of snow, surrounded on both sides by dark green pines, filled Devra with a poignant sense of peace.

The wind whispered through the trees just then, sending snow scattering in a swirling haze of white. Then all was silent, tranquil once more. Silent save for the sweet voices and heartwarming memories echoing in Devra's head. Memories of the gift of love offered by a husband to a wife. A gift that bound them all the more closely, pervading even to their child—and any other who might someday venture upon this exquisite little bridge.

The bridge still looked perfect, despite the harsh Colorado sun and desiccating climate. It suddenly occurred to Devra that her father had continued to maintain the bridge all those years since her mother's death. Was the effort, she wondered, another gift—one of the last ones he could offer in memory of his beloved? Because, as long as Logan MacKay lived, he would continue to care for everything his wife had loved?

He had cared for Culdee Creek that way too, safekeeping it in memory of all the MacKays who had come before and would come after him. Devra had always known of her father's love for this ranch, a love that went far beyond it being solely a means of support or a place to hang his hat.

And it wasn't as if she was insensitive to Culdee Creek herself. It was her home. She had many good memories associated with this place, and always would. She just wasn't so sure she wanted to carry on where her father, and all those other MacKays, had left off.

With a sigh, Devra walked to the edge of the creek where bridge met land. She climbed the steeply curving steps until she reached the relatively flat middle of the bridge. After wiping away the snow that clung to the top railing, she leaned on the support and gazed out on the gray-blue water.

It was so quiet, so peaceful, so beautiful here, almost as if she had happened upon some hidden world within a world. Here, everything seemed so sharp and clear, so alive and ripe with potential, hinting of secrets hovering just beyond one's perception. Devra closed her eyes, straining to pierce that thin veil separating her from what she sensed lay there for the taking. Oh, how she yearned to find the answers, to gain the peace she so desperately needed!

Try as she might, though, the forest, the snowy bridge, the ice-clogged creek, afforded no reply. At long last, the chill beginning to penetrate through her thick layers of clothing, Devra turned and left the bridge. She had found few answers here, no more than she had found back at the house. Still, she felt heartened. The gift of love between her parents, symbolized in such a tangible way by the clean-lined but elegant bridge, had touched her today.

The frigid winds and ever-worsening weather might drive her away for now, but she'd be back.

fifteen

At 3:00 in the afternoon, Thelma headed for home to spend Christmas Eve with her husband. Though she had invited Devra to join them, Devra had said no. Like all the years past, she had come home to spend Christmas at Culdee Creek. With or without other MacKays at her side, she intended to do just that.

Besides, they'd all meet up at St. Michael's this evening for Christmas Eve services, not to mention spend tomorrow afternoon and evening together for the annual ranch Christmas supper. And it wasn't as if she'd be totally alone anyway. Ross was just a short walk up the hill, as were a couple of unmarried hands who made their homes in the renovated bunkhouses down near the barns.

Still, as the day wore on and soon dimmed into a dark, blowing snowstorm, Devra began to regret her decision to go it alone. Though the big evergreen in the living room sparkled with lights and glinting decorations, nostalgic carols and hymns played softly on the radio, and a delicious supper—thanks to Thelma's thoughtful ministrations—warmed in the oven, Devra struggled to find her usual sense of Christmas peace and happy anticipation.

She busied herself with countless tasks, finishing the wrapping of her gifts for Thelma, Ross, and the hands that she'd present at tomorrow's celebration, tidying up the house, watching several Christmas programs, including her favorite, *It's a Wonderful Life*. Eventually, though, an uneasy restlessness forced its way to the forefront. Eventually, she had to face the truth. Without her father, Christmas meant nothing. Absolutely nothing.

Devra knew, of course, that Christmas was really all about God. But though once the celebration of Jesus' birth had been far more important than even the warmth and love of family around her, over the years, as her love and closeness to God had faded, so had that wondrous aspect of Christmas.

That distancing had probably begun the year her mother died. Anne MacKay's passing had ripped open a hole in

Devra's heart so wide that nothing anyone had done—her father included—had accomplished much more than maybe holding the edges of the wound together. But as any physician knew, a wound needed more than holding together to heal. It needed a healthy body and heart, careful nurturing, and a stable, safe environment.

For a long while, her father had been too grief-stricken to offer Devra much nurturing or stability. He had tried—she knew that then as much as now—but he had repeatedly slipped back into a depression that was an effective barrier against others, even though he didn't mean it to be. And though Thelma had tried her best to comfort her, nothing had ever seemed the same again.

Nothing, not even Devra's trust in a merciful, loving God.

She supposed she had deluded herself into thinking she was truly a Christian. Sure, she believed in Jesus Christ, that He was God's Son and God in His own right as well. But He had ceased to matter, save for the occasional lip service she paid Him and the once-yearly church attendance at Christmas services. As much as she had resented Thelma's interference, the old housekeeper had spoken the truth. She didn't carry Christ in her heart anymore.

With an exasperated sigh, Devra rose from the living room couch and turned off the television. She was getting positively somber this evening, with all the regrets and self-recriminations. And her stomach was beginning to growl. Time to get some supper.

For the next fifteen minutes, as the beef and noodle casserole continued to warm in the oven, Devra occupied herself making a salad, toasting some garlic bread, and setting herself a festive table in the dining room. All the while, the wind blew stronger, until powerful, sporadic gusts buffeted the house, and the lights began to flicker occasionally. She peeked out the window as she cleaned up after supper. The storm had turned into a blizzard.

"Great. Just great," she muttered. "At this rate, it doesn't look like we'll be going to Christmas Eve services."

The phone rang, catching Devra halfway between the kitchen and the dining room with her hands full with her plate, glass, and silverware. She hesitated, turned toward the living room where one phone sat, then wheeled around and made a dash for the other phone in the kitchen. By the time she reached the kitchen, freed up her hands, and grabbed for the handset, the phone had stopped ringing.

Caller ID identified it as Ross. Devra punched in his phone number. As she waited for him to pick up, the lights flickered once more and then went out. The phone went dead.

She stood there for a moment in the pitch-black kitchen, waiting for the lights to come back on. Outside, the wind howled and the house rattled and shuddered, and Devra was overcome with the sensation of being swallowed up in a maw of endless darkness. Her breath caught in her throat.

Then she laughed. "Come on, now," she said, chiding

herself. "It's only a snowstorm, for pity's sake. Just find some candles. A little light will shed a whole other perspective on this."

But then Devra couldn't seem to recall where Thelma kept spare candles. She pawed through every drawer and cupboard in the kitchen and still couldn't find anything suitable to use for illumination. After a time, she gave up in frustration. Feeling her way down the hall, Devra made it back to the living room, where she grabbed the afghan off the back of the couch and curled up beneath it in her father's favorite wing chair.

"A fine way to spend Christmas," she groused, beginning to feel sorry for herself. "Daddy's gone. I'm all alone and can't go anywhere, and now not only are the lights out, but the house is starting to feel cold. Maybe they'll find my stiff, frozen body here in the morning."

Devra considered throwing on her boots and jacket and trudging up to Ross's house. Anything was better than sitting here all night in the dark and cold. But even if the possibility of getting lost in that whiteout wasn't deterrent enough, the thought of being considered a crybaby by Ross certainly was. After all these years of being treated like a child, she wasn't about to blow the headway she had recently made with him.

No, she wasn't about to go crying to Ross Blackstone. Let them find her stiff, frozen body here tomorrow, if need be. At least she would've died with what remained of her dignity.

Not that she had much dignity left, at least when it came to Ross. Thelma had said people were talking about them. Had she been making a fool of herself then?

The past six days with Ross had been a crazed whirlwind of emotions, ranging the gamut from loathing and distrust to a giddy happiness. Devra couldn't remember ever feeling such extreme highs and lows, save that summer when she had first met him. It was almost as if . . . as if she were falling in love with Ross all over again.

"No," she moaned, clenching her eyes shut and pulling the afghan up to bury her face. "It's too late. Too late. I'm just so confused, so alone, so hurting right now that I can't think straight. That's all it is."

Guilt flooded her. Her father had only just died, and all she could do was act like some silly girl, mooning after a man who barely gave her the time of day. What in the world was the matter with her, anyway?

Tears of frustration mixed with self-pity spilled down her cheeks. Suddenly, the floodgates broke, and Devra found herself sobbing. The pain she had barely managed to keep at bay the past week flared anew.

"Oh, Daddy, Daddy," she wept. "I miss you. I miss you so much!"

Footsteps sounded on the front porch, and someone rapped hard on the door. Devra's sobs caught in her throat.

She knew it could be only one person on the other side of the door, and it was the one person she desperately didn't want to see right now.

Maybe if she sat there and didn't answer, Ross would think she had gone to bed, and he'd give up and go away. It was cowardly and downright inhospitable, but she didn't trust her emotions right now.

This time a voice joined some pretty hard knocking. "Devra?" Ross called out, piercing even the wind's cacophony. "Devra, I know you're in there. Let me in, will you, before I freeze to death out here!"

With an exasperated sigh, she flung the afghan aside and rose from the chair. The man needed his head examined, going out on a night like this. But she also knew him well enough to know that once he got some fool idea into his head, it was nearly impossible to talk him out of it. And it seemed that tonight he was determined to pay her a visit.

"Come on. Get in here," she muttered, jerking open the door. "Not that you're going to find it much warmer in here than outside."

He stomped in, closed the door behind him, and brushed the snow from his Stetson and thick jacket. "Don't you have any candles? And if you'd bother to get a fire going in Old Bess, you could easily keep the kitchen warm all night."

Old Bess. Devra hadn't given a thought to the cast-iron cookstove. Not that she had ever had much luck with reg-

135

ulating all the various air intake ports to get the proper mix for fire-starting anyway.

"It's not like I know where Thelma keeps everything anymore," she replied a bit testily. "And I hardly get a lot of practice starting fires in cookstoves, either."

"Well, Miss Blue Eyes,"—Ross lifted a flashlight that he flipped on and shone in her face—"I'll bet I can find those candles, and I sure know a thing or two about getting a fire going in Old Bess." He gestured in the direction of the kitchen with the flashlight. "Lead on."

She supposed she should've been irritated with his presumption that she needed or even wanted his help. But at that particular moment she was so glad for something to get her mind off the dismal turn the evening had taken that she was even happy to see him.

It was crazy, putting such importance on the company of a man who had been lost to her a long time ago, Devra thought as she followed the beam of light directed down the hall toward the kitchen. Tomorrow she'd find her way back to sanity and regain the life she had made for herself. But for tonight at least, she didn't really care.

Tonight, all she wanted to do was get through the best way she could.

sixteen

*A*n hour later, the kitchen was toasty warm, five candles were sitting on a plate in the middle of the table, and Devra and Ross were sipping on mugs of steaming tea and munching on cookies she had filched from the stash prepared for tomorrow's Christmas meal. As she sat there across the table from Culdee Creek's foreman, she marveled at what a mere sixty minutes with the right person could do for one's mood. Not that she hadn't enjoyed the company of many others in the years since she had first left home, but nothing—and no one else—had felt so right as sitting here with Ross in a simple kitchen on a cattle ranch in the middle of a Colorado snowstorm.

This was how she had always dreamed it would someday be, with some special man. Cozy, comfortable, and satisfying deep down to the marrow of her bones. Of course, Ross was just the first man who had ever made her feel that way. He wouldn't be the last.

"I didn't want to let you in," Devra said, dropping her gaze to add a spoonful of sugar to her tea. "Thanks to this miserable storm, my evening and all my plans had totally fallen apart, and I wasn't in the best of spirits."

"I kind of figured that might be the case." Ross smiled over at her. "It was getting pretty hard on me too, alone with too much time on my hands to think about things. Though you never liked it much, with Logan always including me in the Christmas Eve celebrations, it made tonight even harder to take with him gone."

"So, your reasons for coming over weren't as altruistic as you tried to make them out to be, is that it?" Devra softened her accusation with a chuckle. "Who would've believed it? Big, tough Ross Blackstone was lonely."

He grinned sheepishly. "Yeah, I was. For Logan, and for you."

She blinked, struck momentarily speechless. "Why for me?" she finally forced herself to ask. "You've never seemed to care about me before. What's changed, save that Daddy's dead?"

"Nothing's changed." He looked away, seemingly staring out the window at the dense whirl of wind-driven snow. "I've always felt the same way about you over the years." He gave a curt, husky laugh. "Nothing's changed since that first day I met you."

Ross turned back, riveting the full intensity of his gaze on her. "I've always loved you, Devra. Always."

She felt like she was in some dream, a dream she had kept buried deep inside her. A dream she rarely allowed to come out into the light of day. Because to risk that was to risk her heart. But hearing Ross speak those words was just as unreal as Devra had always known that dream to be.

She struggled for a reply, and bought herself time by taking a long, careful sip of her tea. "Please don't take this wrong," she said at last, setting her mug back on the table, "but after all these years, after how badly you've always treated me, I find this declaration of love a little hard to take seriously."

"Yeah, I imagine you do." He sighed, looked down, and began to swirl the liquid in his own mug. "Especially after how I hurt you that summer I first came here, when you shared the fact that you loved me."

"Hurt me?" Devra gave a strident laugh. "A pretty mild word for stomping all over my feelings and making me feel like I needed to run home and play with my dolls for another five or six years! You *crushed* me, Ross. Here I was, just beginning to take my first steps into womanhood, and you humiliated me. Do you know how long it took me to feel feminine or pretty or attractive to the opposite sex again? Do you?"

"It was mean, stupid, and cowardly of me. I admit that. I knew it even then. But I was desperate, Devra." He leaned back in his chair and roughly shoved a hand through his hair. "I was twenty-one, fresh out of prison, and I needed the job your father gave me."

"And what exactly did that have to do with me, or justify how you treated me?"

"You were jailbait, honey." His lips curved, and a faraway look softened his gaze. "You were the prettiest girl I'd ever seen, with those big blue eyes, honey blond hair, and your laugh . . . well, every time you laughed, it was like angels had run their fingers across their harp strings. I'd never had a girl as fine as you look at me the way you did.

"It did things to me, stirred feelings, needs, thoughts . . . well, they weren't the kind of things I dared let myself feel for the boss's daughter. But I also knew that if I let you go on much longer, looking at me the way you did, using all those excuses you made up to seek me out, it wouldn't be long before I did something I'd regret. So I decided the only way to save my job, and save us both, was to tell you in no uncertain terms that I wasn't interested."

"So you lied to me."

"I lied the worst lie I'd ever lied in my life."

Listening to him, knowing of his past as she now did,

Devra could almost accept Ross's explanation of why he had so cruelly dashed all her girlish hopes and dreams. But she hadn't remained a girl, and Ross had still persisted in keeping his distance.

"I wasn't jailbait after I turned eighteen," she ground out, all the old anger and confusion churning close to the surface and spilling into her voice. "What was your excuse then? Since you suddenly seem to be full of excuses, I mean."

Sadness filled his eyes. "You wanted to be a doctor, Devra. How could I stand in the way of that kind of dream? I was just a ranch hand, uneducated, a man with a prison record. What did I have to offer you? I loved you too much to ask you to make a choice like that. A choice I was afraid you'd someday regret if you made the choice for me."

He reached over and took her hand. "Look at me, honey. Can you honestly say, knowing what you know now, that you wouldn't have always regretted giving up medical school?"

She looked him straight in the eye because he had asked her to. "Pretty sure of yourself, weren't you, to think I would've given up being a doctor for you?" As she spoke Devra pulled her hand free of his. "Well, if that's really what you thought, I'm glad you didn't ask me. Sooner or later I *would've* regretted marrying you. But not because I gave up medical school for you. No, because I would've finally come to my senses and seen what a selfish, egotistical man you are."

In the flickering candlelight, his rich brown eyes darkened in pain. "And, in some ways you would've probably been right. Maybe I *was* a little egotistical to think you loved me enough to toss aside all your fine plans. Maybe I just wanted you so badly that I convinced myself you wanted me as much." He smiled sadly. "Those dreams were all I had, you know, especially during those times you acted like you hated me. Though I might've deserved it, your coldness hurt. Hurt bad."

"You had no one to blame but yourself!"

"I know, but being the perverse man that I am, it still hurt." Ross sighed. "Look, I know it's too late for us, Devra, and that it's my fault. I know I waited too long, but there never seemed a right time."

His mouth quirked in self-deprecation. "I tried to tell myself you'd come to your senses sooner or later, and when you did, I and Culdee Creek would be here waiting for you. But maybe . . . maybe I was just scared—scared to face the possible end to all my hopes. Scared to tell you I loved you." He leaned back. "I wanted you to know. Know it was never you, but me. Always me."

She gave a shaky laugh. "Some kind of love, I'll say." She pushed back her chair and climbed to her feet. "I think it's time you left, Ross. I've had just about all the revelations I can take tonight."

He stood too. "Yeah, I suppose you have. I'm sorry if I've ruined everything. We were doing pretty well until I opened my big mouth."

Devra shuddered. Tears hovered near the surface, threatening to gush forth in an uncontrollable flow. "Then why did you tell me?" she asked, her voice suddenly low and shaky. "Why?"

"Because I was thinking a lot about your father tonight, and what he said." Ross's lips curved into a sad, wistful smile. "Logan knew all along I loved you. And only a few days before he died, he urged me again to tell you. He said the truth needed telling, one way or another. That it was long past time to end the hurt between us." He released a long, slow breath. "He said it was a gift I owed you, Devra. A gift of love."

A gift of love? How dare he? How dare Ross try to turn what he had done to her into something fine and noble, then think a few pat explanations would make it all come out right?

Rage swamped her, searing a hole clear through to her heart. All the pain, all the shame, all the fury rose up to form a red-hot mist before her eyes. She wheeled around and struck out blindly at him.

The first blow glanced off his cheek. The second he halted in midair.

"Don't, honey," he rasped, his eyes gone black with anguish. "I'm not worth it. I'm not."

Tears spilled down her cheeks. "Yes. Yes, you are," she sobbed, even as she continued to struggle wildly in his grasp. "I hate you. I love you. And I hate that I love you!"

With a groan, he pulled her to him. "I know, honey. I think, deep down, I've always known," he whispered, his mouth but a breath from hers. "Always."

And then, before she could speak again, he kissed her, his lips settling over hers with an aching tenderness. Devra whimpered, grabbed his shirt, and pressed close, arching up on tiptoe to meet him.

Fully, ardently, woman to man.

Then, all too soon, Ross released her and stepped away. His breath ragged, he slowly shook his head.

"I–I should've known better than to come over here tonight. I should go, before this gets out of hand. We can talk more tomorrow." He backed away then, turned, and stalked from the kitchen.

seventeen

he taste of him lingered on her lips, the feel of him pressed close even if only for the briefest, most glorious of moments. Lingered all night as Devra lay in her bed, staring up into the darkness as the storm finally expended its fury and, like some chastened child, crept away. Lingered the next morning as she worked in the kitchen—the electricity back on—peeling potatoes and carrots in preparation for Thelma's arrival.

"We missed you and Ross at the Christmas Eve services last night," the housekeeper said as she finally walked into the kitchen around 10:00 A.M. "Figured the snow storm kept you both on the ranch, though."

"Yes. yes it did," Devra mumbled, ducking her head to hide the sudden warmth that had flooded her face. "But, believe it or not, I really hated not going to Christmas services this year. Considering the near whiteout conditions, though, we just thought it wisest not to try and drive to the Springs."

"We?" Thelma paused in the act of tying an apron around her waist. "So you and Ross talked last night, did you?"

For a fleeting instant, Devra considered dissembling, then gave up the idea. Once before, she had hesitated to confide in Thelma about Ross, and the omission had resulted in catastrophe. Besides, after what had transpired last night, Devra needed all the advice she could get.

"Yes, we talked. When the electricity went out, Ross came over to check on me. He got a fire going in Old Bess, I made some tea, and then we talked." Devra paused to take in a deep breath. "He told me he loved me, Thelma. That he's loved me all along."

"Oh, sweetie, that's wonderful. Absolutely wonderful!" The housekeeper hurried over and took Devra's hands in hers. "If only you knew how many prayers I'd lifted heavenward over the years that that young man would finally get up the courage to tell you how he felt. It does my heart good to know they've finally been answered." She angled her head and studied Devra closely. "So, what did you say? Did you tell Ross you loved him, too?"

Devra couldn't quite meet Thelma's gaze. "Well, I guess. It's just that I've such mixed feelings. I pretty much told him that, too."

"Mixed feelings about what, sweetie? It all seems pretty simple and straightforward to me. You love Ross. He loves you. What's the problem?"

"The problem is . . ." Devra dragged her glance up to meet Thelma's. "The problem is am I out of my mind? Daddy's just died. I have a ranch I don't want and don't know what to do with. And now, out of the blue, Ross tells me he loves me? I mean, what's going on here? A romantic relationship is the last—the *very* last—thing I need right now!"

"Oh, I don't know about that." Thelma shrugged. "Sounds like another one of God's gifts might have just fallen into your lap. Question is, what are you going to do with it?"

Devra made an exasperated sound. "I'm not sure you can call it a gift if I don't see it as one."

"Well, the Lord's view of things is often a lot different from our own. Our task, though, is to learn to see things like the Lord does." The housekeeper led Devra to the kitchen table. "Now, sit, and tell me everything. Especially why you don't see Ross's loving you as a gift. You've never stopped loving *him* all these years, after all. Anyone with half a brain and one good eye could see that. Which, of course," she added with an impish grin, "effectively eliminated both you and Ross up until now."

"Great," Devra grumbled as she took a seat at the table. "So now I'm not only dimwitted but half blind too. It's not that simple, though. I mean, where does Ross get off keeping his feelings secret all these years, while he just goes along making all the decisions for the both of us? He's hidden a lot from me, and I don't find that particularly admirable or honest."

"So now you're afraid to trust anything he says, is that it?"

Trust. Until that moment, Devra hadn't been able to put her finger on the tiny, niggling concern that seemed to scamper off and hide every time she tried to examine it more closely. But Thelma had hit the nail on the head. Ross had kept too many secrets from her. How could she trust him now?

"Yes, I suppose that's it," she said by way of admission. "Why did he choose now, after all these years, to tell me he loved me? It makes no sense, unless . . . unless—"

"Unless it has something to do with him getting his hands on Culdee Creek?"

"I hadn't thought of that until now, but yes, now that you mention it, it does seem the most likely possibility."

"Except that Ross has always loved you, sweetie. He may have made the wrong choice in not telling you of his love until last night, but in the end, I think his heart—if not his head—was in the right place. He was just trying to put you and your welfare ahead of his. And Ross isn't the kind of man to lie, especially about his feelings."

A light of growing conviction shining now in her eyes, Thelma shook her head. "No, something else pushed him to finally tell you the truth. Maybe he, too, has come to the realization that he needed to stop squandering all the gifts God has given him." She smiled softly. "Because he's here, and so are you, and the time is now."

By 3:00 in the afternoon, all the guests began showing up, their cheeks rosy from the cold, stomping snow off their boots, full of pleasant camaraderie and Christmas cheer. Everyone, that is, but Ross.

Just as they were putting the heaping bowls of mashed potatoes, candied carrots, buttered green beans, and platters of honey glazed ham and sliced turkey on the table, Culdee Creek's foreman walked in. Instead of his usual jeans, flannel shirt, and cowboy boots, he was dressed in a dark brown, wool tweed sport coat, black slacks, casual oxfords, and a plaid twill shirt. He looked, to Devra's way of thinking anyway, absolutely scrumptious.

Ross returned everyone's greetings with a smile and nod, then looked to Devra. "Sorry to be late," he said, "but I'd some accounts I was working on, and once I got started, it was hard to stop."

He managed a lame sort of smile. "Can you forgive me?"

At that particular moment, Devra wanted to do a lot more than forgive him. Her earlier doubts vanished into thin air, and all she wanted was to throw herself into his arms and beg him for another kiss. But there were other people around, people, she noticed belatedly, who had all stopped talking to watch them.

Heat flushed her face. "Sure," she mumbled, ducking her head and placing the last bowl of food on the table. "But only if you promise to help with the dishes after supper."

"Well, if that's what it'll take to get back into your good graces, I'm game." He laughed. "Besides, it'll teach me never to be late again. Everyone knows how much I hate doing dishes."

"Almost as much as Ross hates to cook," Chuck offered with a grin. "Just so you know that up front, Devra."

With that, everyone started talking and laughing again. Devra shot Ross a quick, conspiratorial grin, then hurried off to the kitchen. "Anything else that needs bringing to the table?" she asked Thelma, who was just pulling the rolls from the oven. "Or do we have it all out?"

The housekeeper scanned the kitchen. "I think we've got everything but these rolls, and they're coming right now. Go call everyone to the table, will you, sweetie? We want to eat while everything's nice and hot."

The happy gathering didn't have to be asked a second time to gather round, and Thelma walked from the kitchen with a basket of steaming rolls in hand to find everyone expectantly looking her way. She sat, then glanced down to Devra, who sat at the head of the table on her right.

"Will you do the honors, sweetie, and say grace?"

Devra froze. It had been ages since she had said grace, and suddenly, with all eyes on her, her mind went blank. Then she gazed down the length of the table to where Ross sat at its opposite end. Who had placed him there, almost as if he were the father of the household, and she the mother? Thelma, of course. Thelma, who had insisted on assigning everyone a seat this year . . .

Devra managed a weak smile. "Well, I'm a little rusty with praying," she finally said, "so guess I'll just use the one Daddy always used." She folded her hands, bowed her head, and began to pray the only grace she remembered from the Book of Common Worship.

"Lord Jesus be our holy Guest,
Our morning Joy, our evening Rest,
And with our daily bread impart,
Thy love and peace to every heart. Amen."

"Amen," said everyone around the table. Then, after the briefest of pauses, people began grabbing up bowls and platters and shoveling food onto their plates. A pleasant level of noise filled the room, of laughter and good-natured urgings to move the food around the table faster. But it all seemed to fade into the distance as Devra glanced back up and once again met Ross's gaze.

Something arced between them, something deep and warm and so very special. She smiled. He smiled. Then bowls of food were thrust in both of their faces, and they had to return to reality.

It was a wonderful day, spent in the company of friends who, over the years, had become family. Though her father was gone, she knew she'd never come home to barrenness or isolation. She'd never be alone, leastwise when she came home to Culdee Creek.

A few hours after sunset, the Christmas guests began to say their good-byes. Soon, only Thelma, Johnny, Ross, and Devra remained. Devra began scraping the dishes, Thelma and Ross brought in the leftovers from the dining room, and Johnny supervised from the kitchen table.

When all the remaining food was stored in the refrigerator, Devra turned to Thelma. "You and Johnny go on home. Ross and I can do the dishes. He's committed, after all, after his major social faux pas." She shot him an impish grin. "Aren't you, Ross?"

He laughed and nodded. "Sure am. And you can be sure I'll never be late to another Culdee Creek function for the rest of my natural born life."

The housekeeper looked from one to the other and smiled. "Well, okay. I guess that'll be all right. And anything you two decide not to do tonight, just leave for tomorrow. I'll be back bright and early."

They saw Thelma and her husband to the door, watched until they drove away, then reentered the house. Just as soon as the door shut behind them, Ross grabbed Devra and pulled her into his arms. Before she could even say a word, he kissed her long and lovingly.

"Do you know how badly I've wanted to do that, all day and especially since I saw you again?" he asked when he had finally ended the kiss and leaned back. "In fact, I've thought of nothing else since I left you last night."

She frowned. "Then why did you act like you regretted it? I don't remember ever seeing a man hightail it out of a place as fast as you did."

"I almost lost control when I kissed you, honey." As he spoke, Ross tenderly brushed his thumb across her lips. "All those years of longing and dreaming, and I suddenly didn't know myself any longer and didn't like what I was fixing to become."

He sighed. "I wanted you so badly, I was afraid I'd scare you. Or, worse still, that I'd do something that'd be displeasing to God. So, since I didn't feel able to withstand the temptation, I fled it."

She chuckled softly. "Well, you wouldn't have scared me, whatever you did. You're too honorable a man ever to force a woman against her will, and that's the only thing that could've scared me. And I know how strong your faith is, and I would've never wanted you to do anything to jeop-ardize that. Never."

"And what about *your* faith, Devra? How strong is it? Strong enough to withstand temptation?"

"I don't know." She shrugged. "I've never been overly tempted in that department. First, medical school and internship and residency kept me too busy to look very hard for a relationship, and then when I finally had the time, I didn't find a whole lot out there worth pursuing." She reached up and ran a finger down the side of Ross's face. "I realize now why I wasn't looking all that hard. I'd never gotten over you."

Ross smiled, turned his face to her hand, and kissed it. "I'm glad. I can't believe we finally got past all the hurt and misunderstanding, but I'm glad we did. Everything finally seems to be falling into place."

Falling into place. What did he mean by that? Unbidden, the old suspicions raised their ugly heads.

"Well, I wouldn't say *everything.*" Devra leaned back to gaze up into his eyes. "There's still the problem of Culdee Creek, and what to do about it. I haven't made up my mind about that yet, you know."

A tiny furrow formed between his brows. "What do you mean? I thought . . . I thought since we're both in love with each other, it was a natural thing that we'd get married. I know I haven't proposed, but I will, right away, if that's what it'll—"

She covered his mouth with her hand. "No, don't say it. It's too soon. All of a sudden things are moving too quickly. And even if we *did* decide to get married eventually, it's not a given I'd be willing to abandon my practice and move back here. Modern men can move to be with their women, just as often as the woman moves to be with her man, you know."

Ross studied her with grave intensity. "Yeah, I suppose some people do that nowadays. But my life is on this ranch, in the wide-open spaces, doing work with my hands as much as with my mind. And unless I've missed something, I can't recall any ranches in the vicinity of New York City."

Though Devra couldn't envision Ross being happy anywhere but Culdee Creek, his statement still irked her. It smacked of the typical, self-centered masculine expectation that the woman always sacrificed everything for the sake of her man. Well, she had worked too long and too hard to get where she was to toss it all aside, just because some man—even one as handsome and wonderful as Ross Blackstone—asked her to.

She drew back, releasing him. "I guess it just comes down to what you love more, then, doesn't it? Culdee Creek or me?"

His eyes darkened with some indefinable emotion. "That's pretty arbitrary, wouldn't you say, honey? There's always room for compromise. After all, it's not like I'm asking you to give up being a doctor, but just to do your doctoring here instead of in New York."

"And what exactly are *you* willing to compromise, Ross?" Devra asked, her anger rising. "For that matter, what would *you* be compromising, if I'm the one to give up my practice in New York and move back here? Seems to me you'd get it all, with not any change or sacrifice on your part."

"I risk losing you if I don't sacrifice or change. And after all these years of waiting for you and wanting you, that's pretty important to me."

"Then I guess we're at an impasse, aren't we? One of us has to change, or we both lose. But it's all one-sided, any way you look at it."

"I'd change for you if I could, honey." Ross released a frustrated breath. "But it's not just about you. It's also about my love and loyalty to your father, and the ranch he loved. I'm not the kind of man who likes being penned up in tight spaces, but maybe we could work that out somehow. This thing about Culdee Creek and what I owe your father, though . . . well, someone's got to stay here who loves this place, this land, and is willing to carry on the MacKay traditions. And if it's not going to be you, then I guess it's got to be me."

"It always comes back to that, doesn't it? Culdee Creek?" Her voice began to wobble and only with great effort was she able to regain control. "Well, I'm sick to death of hearing about it, of having the whole weight of this place laid on my shoulders. I never, ever, wanted to take over this ranch, and I'm not going to!

"I like my practice. It's very lucrative. And I'm very good at what I do. In New York, people who matter are beginning to notice that. People who have the resources and clout to do big things for me. I wouldn't have those kinds of opportunities in Colorado Springs."

The expression in his eyes sharpened to glittering awareness. "And is that what matters to you now, honey? Power? Prestige? Money? Funny, but I could've sworn that wasn't the reason you went into medicine in the first place."

His words caught Devra up short. Unbidden, her thoughts flew back to that day she had told Ross off when he had teased her about her acceptance to medical school.

"I don't expect you to understand," she had all but shouted at him, her hands on her hips, her stance belligerent and proud. *"What could some old ranch hand know about healing people anyway? But I'm going to be a doctor. I'm going to learn how to fix people's faces, people who've been injured or burnt or just plain born that way. And I don't care if I ever get rich at it or not. All I want to do is make a difference in people's lives!"*

And she *was* making a difference in people's lives, even if in a different sort of way. There was no crime in making money, if you came by it honestly. It was *her* life, and she should be permitted to live it as she wished. She was beginning to wonder, though, if Ross's kind of love wasn't just as restrictive as had been her father's.

"You're making it sound as though I'm in medicine solely for the money," she said. "If that's what you think of me, then you don't know me very well, Ross. And you can't really love what you don't know."

"So now you're saying I don't love you? Is that it, Devra?" He cocked his head, eyeing her. "Or is this some ploy of yours to convince yourself I don't love you, so you can go back to that safe, emotionally isolated life you've been living? The one where you could keep a professional distance and never risk your heart? Because let me tell you one thing, honey. Loving is never safe or easy. That's why none of us would chance it, except for one thing."

"And that one thing is?"

"Life's not worth much without it."

eighteen

*D*evra closed her suitcase, locked it, then pulled it off the bed and placed it beside her other one. She glanced around her bedroom, making sure she hadn't left anything behind. At least nothing valuable, because she wasn't certain she'd ever be returning to Culdee Creek. Once Ross got his hands on the ranch, there certainly seemed no need to.

Five days had passed since the Christmas Day supper and her split with Ross. Five long, painful days of avoiding him and, when she couldn't, refusing to discuss the matter further. No purpose was served by prolonging the agony. Ross refused to compromise, and so did she.

A knock sounded at the door. "Devra? Sweetie?" Thelma's voice tentatively pierced the heavy silence. "May I come in?"

"Sure. The door's unlocked."

She was really in no mood to talk to anyone just now, especially when she'd bet her bottom dollar the housekeeper was going to try one last time to convince her not to leave. But Devra refused to let her anger at Ross color her treatment of others.

Thelma eased her way into the room, shutting the door behind her. She didn't say anything at first, just looked around the room sadly. Finally, though, she met Devra's gaze.

"So you're certain this is what you want?" she asked. "Not only to leave Culdee Creek, but to give it over to Ross?"

Devra could feel the tension begin to rise within her. She clenched her hands into fists, then released them.

"I've said it before. Daddy didn't give me any other choice. So I guess, in the end, it didn't really matter to him if the ranch went to a MacKay or not."

"On the contrary," Thelma said with a disgusted snort. "Seems to me he'd had that figured out pretty good. Considering Ross is at heart more a MacKay than you ever were."

Devra just stared at the other woman. Ross more a MacKay than she? So Thelma had gone over to the other side, had she? But then, if she wanted to keep her job at Culdee Creek, maybe she figured she had to.

The realization, nonetheless, hurt Devra deeply. It also sealed her resolve. There definitely wasn't anything—or anyone—worth coming back home for.

"That's a very unkind thing to say," she muttered, walking to the bedroom's single window to stare outside. "I love Culdee Creek. It'll always be my home. I just won't feel comfortable coming back to visit, that's all."

"Why? Because Ross'll be here?"

Yes, Devra thought, *because I think I'll always love him, as stupid and pointless as that might be, and it'll hurt too much to see him. Better just to put him and the ranch and all the memories back into that dark corner of my mind and try to forget. Try to bury myself in my work, in all the fame and fortune that'll someday be mine.*

Fame and fortune . . . At the recollection of what Ross had said on Christmas Day, tears filled her eyes. *"Funny, but I could've sworn that wasn't the reason you went into medicine in the first place."*

He was right, of course. She hadn't gone into medicine for the money or prestige. But medical school and all the rest of her training had been very costly. She needed to pay her debts.

That was the honorable thing to do, wasn't it? And there was nothing wrong with having her talents recognized and rewarded. She was just making the most of the gifts God had given her.

But this time, Thelma hadn't been implying anything

about Devra squandering her gifts. She had simply been asking about Ross.

"Ross is part of it," Devra replied, continuing to stare out the window. "I won't lie. But that's between him and me."

"Yes, I know that, sweetie." Thelma sighed. "Just know one thing more."

Here it comes, she thought. "And what's that?"

"There'll come a day when you'll regret having let him go. He loves you. He's always loved you. And you've never, ever given that man a fair shake."

The housekeeper didn't linger to hear Devra's response. The next thing Devra knew, the door closed softly behind her. She swung around, but Thelma was already gone.

Devra stared at the closed door. Part of her wanted to run after the woman and protest that her accusations weren't fair. But another part sensed there was a lot of truth in Thelma's words.

She walked to the rocking chair and took a seat. As she slowly began to rock, her mind roiled with frustration, confusion, and doubts. Oh, such doubts!

Was she making the right choice? How in the world could she really be sure? She needed to be sure.

But was there ever any surety in life? If her father's unexpected death hadn't been enough to pull the rug out from under her, nothing ever would. Yet she clung to the illusion that people could control what happened to them.

She had to. She had relinquished all other hope, save that last hope in herself.

Relinquished even the hope that the only surety in life was God, and that she would always be safe in His love.

Her mouth twisted in sad self-deprecation. But wasn't living by false illusions what had led her off her life's true path to begin with? Who was she to imagine she had all the answers, or could ever truly have any real control of her life? Losing her father had slammed open the door of that reality. Only God was in control. If she had even half a brain left in her head, she needed to place her life back into His sure, loving hands.

There was a surety in family too. That they'd always be there for you, even if, for some of them, it was now from in heaven. Her mother. Her father. And, Devra suddenly realized, all the MacKays who had preceded them.

Her glance rested on the antique sewing machine sitting on the small stand in the corner of her room. That had been her great-great-grand-stepmother Abby's sewing machine. Abby, the second wife of Conor MacKay, the man who had first brought Culdee Creek to its present size and prosperity. Even now, Devra could feel a certain comfort in gazing at that old machine, secure in the link connecting her to that wonderful, God-inspired woman.

The old black leather doctor's bag, ensconced between all of Devra's beloved books on her bookshelf, also held a place of honor. It had been her great-great-aunt Beth's bag. Dr. Elizabeth MacKay—Conor MacKay's daughter from an illicit relationship with a Cheyenne Indian, Squirrel Woman—had always been Devra's role model and inspiration.

And the rocking chair. Slowly, lovingly, her hands caressed the smooth arms. She recalled all the times her mother had rocked her in this chair, crooning songs of comfort when she had woken from some bad dream or was ill.

The chair meant so much to her. How could she leave it behind, any more than she could leave Beth's bag or Abby's sewing machine? They'd mean little to Ross, but everything to her.

Devra rose, walked across her room, and out the door. The upstairs hallway was lined with photos of the Mac-Kays. Great-great-uncle Devlin. His wife, Hannah. Beth and her stepbrothers, Sean and Devra's great-grandfather Evan, and her little stepsister, Erin. Evan's wife, Claire, the auburn-haired Scottish beauty. And Beth's great love, the Episcopal priest, Noah Starr.

There were so many of them, all with rich and wonderful stories, of happy, fruitful lives lived on Culdee Creek and its environs. Serving each other. Serving the community. Serving God.

She descended the stairs and entered the living room. There, over the moss-rock and pine fireplace, hung that old painting of a distinguished Scotsman in a blue, green, and black tartan kilt, a basket-hilted sword hanging at his side. Devra knew him to be the family patriarch, Sean MacKay, who emigrated to America in 1825 during the sad times of the Highland Clearances, and who bought the Colorado high plains land that'd eventually become Culdee Creek. They went back even further than that too, back to the village of Culdee in the northernmost part of Scotland. Back to proud, sturdy, courageous Highlanders.

None of them would look very sympathetically on her decision to turn her back on Culdee Creek. She could almost hear them asking her why. What was she so afraid of losing, that she'd walk away from all they had worked so hard to build?

What *was* she so afraid of losing? Devra slipped out of her Italian leather pumps, took a seat in one of the two wing chairs set before the hearth, and pulled up her feet beneath her. It certainly wasn't the right to choose the course her life would take. No one, not her father or Ross, had ever really stood in her way when it came to going to medical school. On the contrary, as misguided as his intent may have been, Ross had even withheld the admission of his love so as not to influence her in any way.

Instead, their issue had always been with the where and why of her life. *Where* she chose to practice, and *why* she had strayed from the path she had first set for herself. In the end, she had already compromised everything that really mattered. All Ross—and her father—had ever tried to do was get her to see that. All they had ever tried to do was offer her that gift of love.

Her glance snared on the glass-enclosed curio cabinet, wherein sat a small bogwood harp. Sunlight drenched its wire strings, sending glinting shards of illumination to reflect on the opposite wall. The MacKay clan harp had been passed down from generation to generation of Scotsmen until, finally, it had been given as a wedding gift to Evan and Claire. That harp, and the worn family Bible that lay beside it, perhaps symbolized most vividly the strong ties that bound all MacKays. Bound them to their glorious Scottish heritage, and to their God.

Joy flooded Devra, flowing through her veins with every beat of her heart. She had feared for a long while now that, in following her dream of becoming a doctor, she'd have to turn her back on her home, heritage, and faith. But now she realized it was that very home, heritage, and faith that had made her the person she was—and the doctor she had always meant to be. To remove any one of those vital parts was to make her a lesser person.

It was why her father had written his will the way he had. It was his last attempt to force her to step back and look at her life. To reevaluate what she really needed as opposed to what she thought she wanted. To see what was truly important for happiness, not in the eyes of man, but in the eyes of God.

Thelma's voice echoed once more in Devra's head. *"The*

Lord won't wait forever, if you insist on squandering what He has so freely and lovingly given. Far better He look with favor on you, proclaiming, 'Well done, my good and faithful servant.'"

Devra looked around the living room once more. These were the gifts she had ignored, squandered even. Her home. Her family. Her heritage. Even her special skills as a doctor. All good gifts, flowing from God through each and every person. Gifts meant to honor the Giver of gifts through unselfish, unstinting service to others.

Gifts she could turn her back on or embrace wholeheartedly, placing her trust where it should've always been—in God.

Devra pulled her legs from beneath her, slipped her pumps back on, and stood. "The time is now, and I am here," she whispered as she crossed the living room and headed for the front door.

It was bright outside, the sun's reflection off the snow intensifying the brilliance. She lifted her hand to shade her eyes, and scanned the area.

Almost as if summoned by her presence, Ross, mounted on a horse, cleared the rise and rode through Culdee Creek's main gate. He was dressed in a dark brown barn jacket, black Stetson, jeans, and boots. To Devra's way of thinking, he looked so much like one of her MacKay ancestors that he might have just ridden out of history. But he wasn't some old-time cowboy. No, he was a here-and-now man—the man she loved.

Heedless of the damage the melting snow would do to her expensive shoes, Devra descended the front porch steps and hurried up the road toward him. Immediately, Ross saw her. For a second or two, he continued to ride on, keeping his horse to a slow trot. Then, as if suddenly realizing what her unexpected appearance meant, with a shout, he urged his horse to quicken its pace.

The big gelding lunged forward, settling into a run.

Dear Readers,

*W*ell, I must say I had a lot of fun writing *All Good Gifts.* It was my first foray into a contemporary setting as a published author, and I'm thinking I just might have to write some additional contemporaries (besides my historicals, of course) from time to time.

As I promised at the end of *Child of Promise,* the fourth book in my Brides of Culdee Creek series (which, for any of you who haven't made that series' acquaintance, are the tales of all those MacKay ancestors who settled Culdee Creek Ranch), my next book for my publisher Fleming H. Revell will be a story about the original MacKay ancestors back in Scotland in those wild, glorious times when real men wore kilts, claymores flashed in defense of clan and honor, and bagpipes skirled their plaintive, poignant songs. You'll learn more about the ancient village of Culdee, introduced in *Lady of Light* (book 3 in the Brides of Culdee Creek series) and hear the tale of how the family clarsach first found its home with the MacKays.

That book, still untitled, should be out sometime in 2004.

I'm really looking forward to writing it. In the meanwhile, check out my web site at http://www.kathleenmorgan.com for updates on all my upcoming books.

Kathleen Morgan

P.S. I'm always happy to hear from readers. To be included on a mailing list (either postal mail or e-mail) with updates on future books, write to Kathleen Morgan at P.O. Box 62365, Colorado Springs, CO 80962 (and be sure to enclose a self-addressed, stamped business-sized envelope for my newsletter) or e-mail me at kathleenmorgan@juno.com. Overseas readers need, instead of stamps, to include international reply coupons purchased at their local post office to cover the cost of postage.

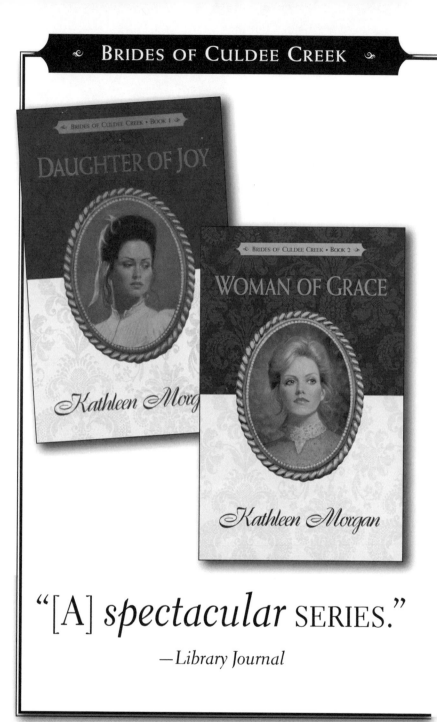

BRIDES OF CULDEE CREEK

BRIDES OF CULDEE CREEK • BOOK 1

DAUGHTER OF JOY

Kathleen Morgan

BRIDES OF CULDEE CREEK • BOOK 2

WOMAN OF GRACE

Kathleen Morgan

"[A] *spectacular* SERIES."

—*Library Journal*

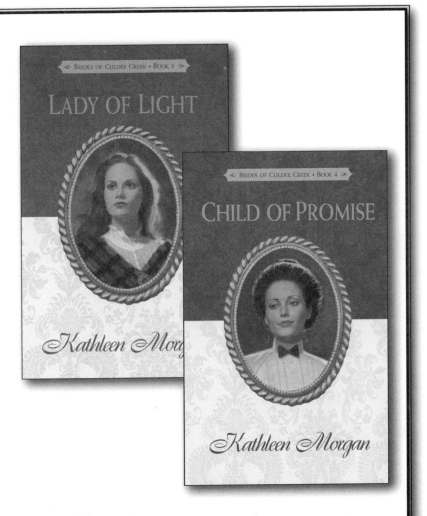

"Kathleen Morgan puts a new spin on romance!
Her characters are passionate and memorable!"
—*The Literary Times*

"A marvelous storyteller."
—*Romantic Times*